Two Dogs

Also by Patrick C. Walsh

The Mac Maguire detective mysteries

The Body in the Boot

The Dead Squirrel

The Weeping Women

The Blackness

23 Cold Cases

The Match of the Day Murders

The Chancer

The Tiger's Back

The Eight Bench Walk

Stories of the supernatural

13 Ghosts of Winter

The Black Vaults Experiment

All available in Amazon Books

Patrick C. Walsh

Two Dogs

The sixth 'Mac' Maguire mystery

Garden City Ink

A Garden City Ink ebook
www.gardencityink.com

First published in Great Britain in 2017
All rights reserved
Copyright © 2017, 2018, 2020 Patrick C. Walsh

A CIP record for this title is available from the British
Library
ISBN 9780993280085

Cover art © Patrick S. Walsh 2017
Garden City Ink Design

'A Native American elder once described his own inner struggles in this manner: Inside of me there are two dogs. One of the dogs is mean and evil. The other dog is good. The mean dog fights the good dog all the time.

When asked which dog wins, he reflected for a moment and replied...'The one I feed the most.'

George Bernard Shaw

For Patrick

How it started

He nodded at the three men as he sat down. Only the bald-headed man seated opposite was important. The two men standing on either side of him were just highly paid servants. They were all dressed in dark suits and ties and it might have been just another business meeting except for the fact that they were seated at a table that stood in the middle of a large grassy field. Overhead the sky was blue with huge white fluffy clouds scudding by.

He hadn't known where they were taking him. He was picked up in a quiet backstreet where he was blind-folded and bundled into the back of a car. A half an hour later and here they were, wherever it was.

'You've verified it then?' the bald-headed man said dispensing with any attempt at small talk.

'I have. A top expert has vouched that it's genuine,' he replied. 'He examined it himself just a few days ago.'

He pushed a document towards him but the bald-headed man didn't even acknowledge its existence. One of the servants picked it up and read it carefully. When he'd finished, he nodded to his master.

'When can I expect delivery?' the bald-headed man asked.

He noticed a bird of prey circling overhead and he thought how like the bald-headed man it was; efficient, cold blooded and totally heartless. He'd known that this job would be a challenge and that any mistake could prove to be costly, fatal even. It was a high stakes game but that only made it all the more exciting.

However, he had absolute confidence in his own abilities. There would be no mistakes.

'There's the small matter of the down payment first,' he said.

Servant number two laid an attaché case on the table and opened it up. He looked at the thick wads of high

1

denomination notes inside and did a quick mental calculation. It looked correct. He shut the case and placed it on the ground next to his seat.

'One million euros,' the bald-headed man said, 'with another three million on delivery as agreed.'

'Everything has been prepared and you can expect delivery within the next two weeks.'

He saw avarice in the bald-headed man's steely eyes, avarice and a sort of need.

He must really want it desperately, he thought, and, for a brief moment, he considered upping the price. Then he reminded himself of whom he was dealing with and dismissed the notion.

'There'll be no loose ends, I hope?' the bald-headed man asked.

He knew exactly what he meant by this.

'I never leave any loose ends. It will be an absolutely clean job.'

The bald-headed man gave him the briefest of smiles. He stood up and walked off without another word. His two servants followed behind like pet dogs.

He was blindfolded again and, as he was being driven back to the city, he thought about the plan that they had just set in motion. The clock was now ticking and before long the thread of someone's life was going to be cut. A murder had just been agreed upon but that didn't bother him in the slightest.

After all it was just the cost of doing business.

Chapter One

'Oh, it's such a lovely day today,' Amrit said as she looked out into the back garden.

Mac could only agree. It was nearly mid-July and the sun was shining brightly. It had been forecast to get even warmer over the next few days. Unlike him his nurse was dressed for the hot weather. Her sari was made from a very light material which hung loosely around her. It was of a light blue colour with an intricate embroidered design in a darker blue. Her sandals were also light and encrusted with stones that sparkled as she walked. He had to admit that it suited her.

He looked down at his long trousers and shoes. He saw a lot of men going around in shorts and sandals these days and they looked so comfortable in the heat. He'd actually bought a pair of both not long ago. He'd put them on in the privacy of his bedroom and then looked at himself in the mirror. The words 'big girl's blouse' leapt into his mind and a few seconds later he was back in his long trousers and shoes. For the sake of everyone else he decided that his only concession to the heat should be a short-sleeved shirt with no jacket.

'Where is it that Bridget's gone again?' Amrit asked.

'They've gone to Cyprus, somewhere called Larnaka. It's well over thirty-five degrees there at the moment so it's a bit hotter than here. She always did love the sun so hopefully she and Tommy are having a relaxing time. God knows that they've both earned it.'

Mac had never been to Cyprus and had no plans to go anytime soon. Unlike his daughter and her boyfriend, he didn't like it when it got too warm. This was probably due to his West of Ireland heritage where the very hottest of days might still be described as 'fresh' without any hint of understatement. The winds howling in from the North Atlantic saw to that.

3

'Oh, if I know Bridget, she'll be having a whale of a time. She always knew how to enjoy herself,' Amrit said.

'In what way?' Mac asked.

He was interested as Amrit must have seen a different side to his daughter. When they had first met, she'd been a senior nurse and Bridget had been a junior doctor fresh out of training.

'Ah, now that would be telling, wouldn't it? Anyway, are you going to go out today?' Amrit asked neatly changing the subject.

'Yes, I thought that I might as well go to the office and see if there's any mail. I doubt there will be but I haven't been there for a while so you never know. I'm meeting Tim for a drink later and I can always dawdle away a few hours in David's Bookshop, I suppose.'

'That sounds like a plan then. It would be such a shame to be stuck indoors on such a nice day,' she said with a smile.

Mac felt that his nurse was trying to make a point. He was still recovering following the Natasha Barker case. He'd injured his back while saving her after she had tried to hang herself. That had cost him six weeks spent flat on his back in bed. It had been hard on him having to cope with both the pain and the boredom although he reminded himself that it hadn't all been boring. Although he was now up and about again, his doctor had told him to take it easy for a while. However, he had a feeling that his nurse thought he'd been taking it a bit too easy lately.

He sighed. She was probably right as usual. He knew that he that he needed to be getting out more. So, he'd go to his office. He didn't really expect there to be any mail but it was something to do.

His favourite taxi driver Eileen dropped him opposite his office. He thought it as well to get a taxi into town as he would be meeting Tim for a drink later on. The trip was just long enough for him to catch up with all of the latest local news. Eileen knew pretty much everything that went on in Letchworth and Mac sometimes felt the urge to ask her to go around the block a few times so that he could hear more.

Tim's antiques shop was next door to his office but he could see from the other side of the street that the lights were off and the 'Closed' sign was on display. Tim was away doing some furniture renovation at a client's home and Mac hoped that he wouldn't be delayed in getting back. He was looking forward to his session at the Magnets with his best friend.

He could also see that someone had parked a massive great car right outside his office. He didn't look at it too closely as he was muttering under his breath at the extra few yards that he'd have to walk to go around it.

He was about to go inside when he noticed that the little brass plate by the door looked like it needed a bit of a clean. He had some paper tissues in his pocket and he breathed on the plate and then rubbed it until it gleamed. He smiled as the words 'The Garden City Detective Agency' glittered in the sunlight.

It was a strange sort of agency, he thought, having just the one detective and him being an old crock at that.

His office was at the end of the hallway and, in the dim light, he could make out that someone was standing outside his door. As he came closer a young man turned to him.

'Are you Mr. Maguire?' he asked in a northern accent.

'Yes, that's me. Come in,' Mac replied as he unlocked the office door.

It was hot and stuffy inside so Mac went and opened a window. This didn't help much as there was hardly any breeze.

Mac parked his crutch in the corner, sat down and took a good look at the young man. He was dressed in a grey lounge suit, white shirt and grey tie and he was holding a grey peaked cap in his hand. Someone's

5

chauffeur obviously. He definitely wasn't dressed for the heat and his face had a light sheen of sweat on it.

'How can I help you?' Mac asked.

The young man looked somewhat embarrassed as he asked, 'Are you sure that you're really Mr. Maguire? The Mr. Maguire who's a private detective?'

Mac noticed that he was looking with some disbelief at his crutch as he said this. This didn't exactly put the young man in Mac's good books.

He testily replied, 'I assure you that I am indeed Mr. Maguire the private detective. I'm fairly sure that I've got my birth certificate around here somewhere if you want to a take a look?'

He shook his head.

'No, that's okay,' the young man said totally oblivious to the sarcasm in Mac's voice. 'You're to come with me then.'

He turned and headed for the door.

'Whoa! Hold on, I'm not going anywhere until I know what you want me for.'

'I've been told not to say too much as my boss wants to tell you everything herself.'

'And your boss is...?'

The chauffeur got a card from his pocket.

'She said to give you this if you needed any persuasion.'

Mac scrutinised the card. It had a photo of a woman in her forties and the legend, 'Miss Cathy Conyers, Actress' in fancy type along the bottom. She looked vaguely familiar but Mac couldn't quite place her.

'Am I supposed to know her or something?' he asked.

The chauffeur was visibly shocked.

'She's Maggie Martin, you know from Eastdale Street.'

Mac knew that 'Eastdale Street' was the name of a very popular and long running television soap opera but that was as far as his knowledge went. He vaguely remembered seeing the programme once some years before when visiting one of his wife's relatives. This relative had unfortunately been besotted by the show and her whole life had revolved around it. She wouldn't miss an episode for anyone, not even when family were visiting. Afterwards Mac had said a little prayer of thanks to God that his wife Nora had never been afflicted in the same way.

'So, what does Miss Conyers want with me?' he asked.

'I'm under strict instructions not to say any more than I have to,' the young man replied, 'but she lives less than fifteen miles from here and, if you come with me, then you can find out for yourself.'

Mac hadn't planned on going back to work just yet but he found that he was becoming intrigued.

'Okay, I'll go but only if I can sit in the front and you don't wear that stupid cap while I'm in the car.'

It was a deal the young chauffeur was more than happy to make.

He didn't have to tell Mac which car to get into as a silver coloured Bentley Mulsanne was parked right outside. It was also the very same car that Mac had been muttering about having to walk around just a few minutes before. The chauffeur opened the door for him then removed the seat cover and motioned for Mac to climb in. Despite himself, he was impressed as he stepped inside.

The chauffeur drove smoothly towards the motorway while Mac looked over the interior of the car. The seats were beige leather and so comfortable that he could have sworn his back had given a little sigh of relief as he sat down. The dashboard, made of a light gleaming wood, had enough dials for a medium sized airplane. It was also blessedly cool inside the car.

No wonder, Mac thought. The air conditioning unit was probably as big as his car's engine.

He looked at the speedometer as they joined the motorway. They were doing over ninety yet it felt more like forty. He smiled as he thought of his little green Almera straining to get past seventy if the road was even slightly uphill.

Yet for all that he knew he would never buy such a car, even if he had the money. A car like this was a statement, a neon sign letting the world know that you had made it. Mac felt that he didn't need to make any statements and, if he was honest, he was quite fond of his little car. They'd been through a lot together.

'By the way why did you need to take the cover off the seat before I sat down?' Mac asked.

'The cover is for the dog,' the chauffeur replied. 'When it's in the car that's where it sits. Miss Conyers always sits in the back.'

Mac couldn't think of anything to say by way of reply.

They came off the motorway, took the Hertford Road through Old Welwyn, and then took the Kimpton Road for a few miles more. The gently rolling countryside was beautiful and, although man made, the ancient green fields and hedges felt organic and very natural. Many of the houses they passed were old and weathered and seemed to belong there as much as the rocks and trees. And there were trees, lots of trees.

Mac had a sad moment as he was reminded of the first time that he'd driven his wife Nora into Hertfordshire many years before. He remembered her saying that the people here must really love trees. They'd always lived in the centre of big cities before that. First in Birmingham, where they were born and grew up surrounded by factories and the clanging sounds of metal-bashing, and then the hustle and bustle of London for a few months while they found somewhere to live. Mac hadn't known it at the time but Nora had always harboured a secret wish to live in the country. She told him later that she'd made her mind up to live somewhere in Hertfordshire on that very first drive.

8

The Bentley turned off into a narrow, tree lined road that ran between more green fields. Mac had never been this way before and he thought how much Nora would have enjoyed the scenery. A sign at the next junction said 'Ayot St. Lawrence and Shaw's Corner' and indicated that they should turn left. Mac was even more intrigued. Shaw's Corner had been the home of the playwright George Bernard Shaw and was now a museum. He and Nora had often talked about visiting the place where so many of their favourite plays had been written but, unfortunately, it was just one of the numerous things that they had never quite managed to get around to doing.

Mac only caught a glimpse of the great man's house as they sped by. The Bentley turned right at the corner and a quarter of a mile or so down another twisty narrow lane they pulled up outside an electric gate that opened when the chauffeur held his hand against a screen.

A bit over the top, Mac thought, using fingerprints to open a gate in Hertfordshire.

Behind the gate there stood a huge half-timbered cottage that Mac guessed must be at least three or four hundred years old. It somehow looked out of place with the modernity of the electric gate and the high security fence that surrounded the property.

After basking in the coolness of the Bentley's air conditioning the heat outside felt as if someone had just opened an oven door. He followed the chauffeur into the house and was told to wait. The house was thank-fully as cool as the car had been.

He looked around and took a flying guess that Miss Conyers was not into minimalism. Expensive frippery cluttered each and every corner of the large room. The frippery was only exceeded by the number of pictures of the actress herself in various poses. He had the sinking feeling that he and Miss Conyers might not get on. This was confirmed when the lady herself made an entrance.

'Ben, you can go,' she ordered grandly.

A cloud of expensive perfume washed over Mac making him feel mildly nauseous. The chauffeur disappeared but Mac couldn't help noticing that he looked a bit annoyed for some reason.

She gestured for him to sit next to her on the sofa but she wasn't too put out when he sat in the armchair opposite instead. She wore a loose wrap around dress and, although probably now the wrong side of forty, she was still a very handsome woman. Mac guessed that she must have been quite beautiful when she was younger.

She looked Mac over and he could see her eyes settle on the crutch that he was holding in his right hand.

'Oh, I'm sorry. I didn't know you were...' she left the sentence unfinished.

Mac finished it for her.

'...disabled? Yes, I have been for some time now.'

'Will you be up to it, carrying out an investigation?' she asked looking as though she might need some convincing.

'Yes,' he replied grumpily without giving any further explanation.

'Well, Mr. Maguire you know best. I'll bet you're wondering why you're here?'

He nodded but said nothing. He just wished that she'd get on with it.

'I only ever have the best,' she continued, 'so, when I needed a detective, I knew that it had to be you. Mac Maguire, the famous murder specialist. I was especially impressed when I read about how you saved that poor girl Natalie from hanging. That was so brave of you. As you can see, I've done my homework.'

In fact, the girl's name had been Natasha but he couldn't be bothered to correct her. He just wanted her to get on with it.

'What can I do for you, Miss Conyers?'

'Oh, please call me Cathy,' she replied with a cheesy smile. Her face then suddenly turned sad. 'I'm afraid that it's my poor little girl, she's gone. I must admit that I've been worried sick since she disappeared and I desperately need your help to find her. You will help me, won't you?'

Chapter Two

Mac was suddenly interested. A missing girl, he hadn't expected anything so serious. Might he finally have a case that he could get his teeth into?

'How long has she been missing?' he asked sitting forward.

'Just over two days now. My poor little Charmaine, I do worry so about her.'

'I take it that you've told the police?' Mac asked.

'Of course, they said they'd do their best but I knew they were just fobbing me off,' she said giving him a hurt look. 'I don't think they took me seriously at all.'

He was puzzled as to why this should be.

'How old is Charmaine?' he asked.

'Let's see, she must be six by now.'

Six! His heart fell into his boots. He began to smell a rat or at least something furry.

'Have you got a photo?' he asked his grumpiness growing by the second.

She got up and took a framed photo from the wall and brought it over to him.

'That's her,' she said as she theatrically wiped away a tear.

Mac wondered what he'd done to deserve this. He wished fervently that the chauffeur might have arrived a half an hour later. Instead of being here he might have been nicely tucked up in David's with a coffee and a good book.

The photo had only two subjects; Miss Conyers, giving the camera a stage smile, and the huge German Shepherd that she was holding on a leash.

Charmaine was a dog.

He sighed. When he signed up to be a private detective, he hadn't been exactly sure what the work might entail but he was fairly certain that the job description didn't include finding missing pets. He paused and, although his immediate reaction was to just get up and walk out, he decided to make his response as diplomatic as possible.

'Miss Conyers, I'm a private detective not a dog catcher. I have absolutely no expertise in that area and so I don't think that I'm going to be able to help you.'

He got up to go.

'I know where the dog is,' she said sharply.

The hard edge to her voice surprised Mac. Her face had become harder as well.

Am I now seeing the real Miss Conyers at last? Mac wondered.

'Well, if that's the case then you don't need me, do you?' he stated and once again turned towards the door.

'At least I'm fairly sure I do but I need you to confirm it. It won't take you more than a couple of hours and I'll pay,' she said with a smile.

She seemed certain that mentioning money would do the trick.

'I don't need your money, Miss Conyers. Goodbye,' Mac said as he started to turn the door handle.

She was surprised by his reaction and quickly decided to try another tack.

'Wait, just wait,' she pleaded and left the room.

Mac frowned. He wanted to walk right out of there but he realised that, unfortunately, he needed a lift back. Fifteen miles is a long way to walk. He decided that he might as well wait and see what she had up her sleeve.

While he waited, he walked around the room as his back was starting to feel a bit stiff. In an alcove he noticed a small painting that hung in splendid isolation. It had a thick pane of glass in front of it but he couldn't make out much detail as the alcove was in deep shadow. He didn't hear her come back.

'Want a look?' she asked from behind him.

She pressed a switch and the painting sprang to life.

13

Mac was immediately captivated. The painting was of a young naked woman and showed her from the waist upwards. Her head was tilted to one side and her eyes were closed. She appeared to be in some private and rapturous moment. Around her colours swirled ominously. It was both erotic and tender with a splash of something sinister.

'She's good, isn't she?' she asked.

'I'm no expert but yes, I'd say she is. Who painted her?'

'Munch, the same Munch who painted The Scream,' she replied proudly.

'I'm impressed. Tell me is that the real thing?' he asked, fairly sure that it must be a copy.

'Yes, it's the real thing. I know that it's worth a lot of money but I like to have it where I can see it. It's really special to me.'

Mac wondered if there might be a little more depth to the actress than he'd given her credit for so far.

'Here,' she said as she gave him a cheque for five thousand pounds. 'I've left the payee's name empty. If you don't want the money then just enter the name of your favourite charity. Think of all the need in the world, Mr. Maguire,' she said with a winning smile as she waved the cheque under Mac's nose.

He sighed once again. She had him and she knew it.

He reluctantly took the cheque and said, 'Okay, where's the dog then?'

'She'll be at my ex-husband's place. We split up just over six months ago and it wasn't exactly amicable. He was willing to let me have just about everything if I let him have the dog.'

'Why didn't you then?' Mac asked.

'Because he loved that bloody dog more than he loved me. That's why,' she acidly replied.

'Okay, so let's get this clear. All I have to do is confirm whether your ex-husband has the dog or not. Is that right?'

'If he does have Charmaine then you'll need to get a photo to prove it but, other than that, yes. Once I know he's definitely got her then I can get my lawyers involved. With any luck he'll end up in prison.'

Mac was suddenly glad that he'd never married an actress, not that he'd ever had the chance anyway.

'If you give me your husband's details then I'll get on with it,' Mac said feeling the need to get out of there as soon as possible.

'I've put it all on here,' she said as she handed Mac a sheet of paper. 'My mobile number's on there too.'

Mac quickly read it. He then folded it and put it in his pocket.

Seeing Mac's lack of surprise, she asked, 'I take it that you're not into rock music then?'

'Not really, more baroque classical and blues music. I take it that your husband's a rock musician then?'

'Of course, he is. I'm really surprised that you haven't heard of Johnny Kinsella. He's the lead singer in Black Lead,' she said.

Mac knew who they were. They were originally from Birmingham and he'd seen them playing once in a local club a couple of times many, many years ago. He hadn't liked them then and, although they were now world famous, he still didn't like them.

'I'm leaving for Manchester soon as I start filming again tomorrow,' she said. 'Call me on my mobile number as soon as you know something. Leave a message for me if it's switched off, I want to know as soon as possible what's happened to Charmaine.'

Mac promised that he would and left. The heat hit him once again as he walked outside but he breathed in deeply none the less.

He was just glad to get out and to get away from the fripperies, the perfume and the paranoia.

Chapter Three

The chauffeur was waiting in the car outside. The engine was running and he was ready to drive him back to his office. Mac gratefully climbed into the cool interior. He thought that he might as well try to get a little more background information about Cathy Conyers while he had the young man all to himself.

'What's your name by the way?' Mac asked as the Bentley glided down the narrow country lanes.

'It's Ben, Ben Meeks.'

'Well Ben, how long have you been driving her highness around?'

'Only six months or so, ever since she and Johnny split up. I used to do the gardens before that.'

A promotion then, Mac thought, and wondered what else his duties might entail.

'Do you two get on alright?'

The young man looked at him suspiciously.

'Yes of course. Why? What did she say?'

Mac used one of his best weapons; silence. He just gave Ben his best look and he started crumbling instantly.

'Well, we've had our ups and downs but we're okay, most of the time anyway. I know that she's upset but it wasn't my fault the bloody dog disappeared,' he said defensively.

'Tell me about it,' Mac said.

'It was last Friday and the boss was up north filming. So, there was just me and Jimmy in the house. Jimmy's taken over in the garden from me.'

'Why don't you drive her up to Manchester?'

'She doesn't like long car trips. She says that it makes her feel sick and anyway the traffic can be terrible on the M6. So, she takes the train instead. She says that she can study her lines better on the train. She and Eleanor go through them together.'

'Eleanor, who's she?' Mac asked.

'Eleanor Tarbridge, she's Cathy's personal assistant. She's been working for Cathy for over twenty years now. It's like they're joined together at the hip, them two.'

If that was the case then Mac wondered at her not being present during his interview with the actress.

'So, where's she now, this Eleanor?'

'Probably around Bermuda somewhere I should think,' Ben replied. 'She's just gone off on a cruise with her husband. It's their thirtieth anniversary and Cathy bought it for them as a present. It was my idea really and I booked it up for them and everything.'

From his expression Mac gathered that he felt he wasn't getting enough credit for his generous actions.

'Does she live in the house with Cathy?'

'Eleanor? No, she and her husband live in Welwyn but she might as well for the amount of time that she spends there.'

It was obvious that the chauffeur wasn't a fan of Miss Conyers' assistant.

'Okay, carry on,' Mac said.

'Anyway, that day Alice, the cook, had a day off. I was outside helping out Jimmy in the back garden, we all muck in as necessary, so I hadn't heard the car pull into the front drive. The first I knew was when I saw a shadow moving about in the house. I was nearly going to call the police but, when I got a bit closer, I could see him quite clearly through the big back window. It was Johnny and he had a dog lead in his hand. I went back to doing the gardening and pretended that I hadn't seen him.'

'Why?'

'Christ, you should have seen the rows him and Cathy used to have. They used to throw things at each other

18

and once I even saw punches thrown. I just didn't want to be involved.'

'Was Johnny knocking Cathy about then?' Mac asked.

'No, if I'm honest it was Cathy throwing the punches on that occasion but I mean he bites the heads off snakes, doesn't he? It makes me feel sick just thinking about it,' Ben said with a disgusted expression.

'I thought that was just a myth, him biting the heads off snakes on stage.'

'Myth or not he's a scary guy.'

Mac wondered if the chauffeur had another reason to fear Johnny.

'Were you scared of him because you're sleeping with his ex-wife?' he asked bluntly.

'I don't know who told you that but no, we're not sleeping together.'

Mac thought that his tone of voice had been somewhat wistful and he could understand that. After all his employer wasn't bad looking and he supposed that the fact that she was really rich didn't make her any less attractive.

'When I saw him in the house, I must admit that I was a bit worried that he might start on me,' Ben continued. 'Once, a couple of months ago when he'd had a few, he accused me of being responsible for him and Cathy splitting up. He was quite nasty about it too. I honestly don't know where he could have gotten that idea from.'

'So, what did Johnny do?' Mac asked.

'He was okay this time actually. All he did was ask me and Jimmy if we'd seen the dog. Sharmy he calls it.'

'And had you?' Mac asked.

The young man shook his head.

'I took it out for its morning walk at nine and then let it loose in the garden. The garden's massive but, with all the fences, I knew it couldn't get out. So, when I didn't see it around, I didn't worry too much. It always turns up when it's hungry.'

'I take it that you don't like the dog much?'

'What makes you think that?' Ben said defensively.

'You call the dog 'it' and not 'her'.'

'Well, it's true I suppose. That dog's too big for my liking, scary. I've never got on with dogs. I must have been bitten when I was a kid or something.'

Mac wondered at such a well-built young man finding so many things in life 'scary'.

'So, what happened then?'

'Johnny had a look around the garden and, while he was doing that, I had a peek around the front.'

'Why?'

'To see if the electric gate was shut. He was always leaving it open when he lived there.'

'I'd have thought that such a fancy gate would shut automatically, wouldn't it?' Mac asked.

'It does but if you park within six feet or so then the gate won't operate,' Ben explained. 'A safety feature, I suppose. Anyway, Johnny had the bad habit of parking too close to the gate so it wouldn't shut. It used to drive Cathy nuts.'

'And was it open?' Mac asked.

'Yes, I closed it manually to make sure the dog didn't escape and then went back to the gardening.'

'But the dog might have already gone, mightn't it?'

The young man gave this some thought and then conceded the point with a shrug of his shoulders.

'Did you see Johnny leave?' Mac asked.

'No, I looked around fifteen or twenty minutes later and he was gone. I presumed that he'd found what he was looking for.'

'Does your boss always film on Fridays?'

'Yes, she's at the studios without fail every Wednesday to Saturday,' Ben replied. 'She leaves on Tuesday afternoon and comes back late Saturday night.'

'So, Johnny would have known that she'd be away?' Mac asked.

'Absolutely.'

'I take it that Johnny got in the same way you did, using his fingerprints?' Mac asked.

'It's the only way there is to get in.'

'So, why didn't your boss have his fingerprints deleted from the system when they divorced?'

'She would have if she knew how,' Ben said. 'I'm afraid that technology isn't her strong point.'

'Couldn't you have done it?'

The young man hesitated and chewed his lip.

'I offered to but...the gates are all part of the same security system, the burglar alarms and so on.'

Mac thought that he was beginning to get a handle on the relationship between the actress and her chauffeur. Miss Conyers obviously didn't trust the help with something as important as the security systems. Mac was already tired of the case and hoped that Johnny Kinsella did have the dog. One photo and his involvement would be at an end.

He couldn't wait.

Ben dropped him off outside his office. It had started to rain sharply so Mac hurried into the building. Even the rain was warm and, rather than cooling things down, it just made the air more humid. He was surprised to see another figure shuffling around in the dim hallway. Someone else was waiting outside his office door. Mac was beginning to wonder if he should get a 'Queue here' sign installed.

As the figure turned, he could see a flash of white from a dog collar and recognised his parish priest, Father Pat Curran. Father Pat was in his early forties and had been running the parish for over four years since the old priest had died. He'd been a real favourite of his late wife who had helped in the church with the flowers, cleaning and giving readings during mass.

Mac immediately started feeling a bit guilty. He hadn't darkened the church's doors for quite a while now.

21

'I'm sorry that I haven't been to mass much, Father,' he said as he opened the door, 'but...'

'Oh, it's not about that Mac,' the priest said in his thick Cork accent.

Mac turned and he could see a look of real worry on the priest's face. He held the door open and gestured for him to sit down.

'So, what can I do for you Father?' Mac asked stumped as to why a priest might need his help.

'I've just come from the police station and, oh Mac, what a bloody mess!'

The priest's face suddenly crumpled. He held his head in his hands and started crying. This was totally unlike him and it was immediately obvious to Mac that something really serious had happened.

'Tell me what's happened Father. I can't help if you don't tell me,' he said anxiously.

Father Pat pulled himself together and simply said, 'I can hardly believe it myself but the police, they think I killed a man. Oh Mac, they think that I'm a murderer!'

Chapter Four

It was turning into an incredibly surreal day and Mac's first reaction was to wonder for a moment if he wasn't having one of the weird lucid dreams that his pain medication often triggered. Once he'd convinced himself that it was all real, his second reaction was to feel shocked. In fact, he couldn't have been more shocked if he'd stuck his finger in an electric socket.

The reason he was so surprised was that Father Pat was just about the gentlest man he'd ever met and the thought of him even raising his voice, let alone being involved in a violent act, was totally inconsistent with everything he knew about him. Mac had never been a particularly religious man, however, Father Pat had been there for him with a kind word during the dark times after his wife's death. Mac would never forget that.

'Who are you supposed to have killed?' Mac asked.

'My next-door neighbour, Albert Ginn. May God forgive me, Mac. I have never truly hated a man in my life, but if I had, Albert Ginn would have been that man.'

'Why Father?'

Mac was really interested and wondered what this neighbour must have been like to make such a mild-mannered man as Father Pat dislike him so.

'He was a cruel man who only got joy from other's misfortunes and he was malicious with it. He only smiled when some nasty joke of his worked out. I'm convinced that there isn't a person in the whole of Letchworth who could honestly say that they liked Albert Ginn.'

'So, why do the police think that you killed him? And anyway, I thought that you lived in the presbytery next to the church. So how come that you're now living next door to the neighbour from hell?' Mac asked.

'I'll tell you. Three months ago, they found cracks in the presbytery's walls and they told me that I'd have to move out for a while as they had to carry out some structural repairs. The parish owns a house in the street next to the church. We bought it at a good price some time ago from a former parishioner and we used it to house the newly ordained priests while they waited for a parish of their own. In all conscience I knew I had to move there as I couldn't cause the parish any unnecessary expense but I have to admit that I was dreading it. I've had a few run-ins with Mr. Ginn in the past and I had a fair idea of what life would be like living next door to such an odious man.

The house was empty because the diocese wouldn't allow any new priests to live there after Father Xavier had his eyebrows blown off. Another of Mr. Ginn's little jokes. We've tried to sell the house several times but we never even got a single offer. My neighbour had put a one-man blight on the whole area and so I was stuck. I prayed to God to give me the strength to endure what I knew would be a testing period.

Even so it was far worse than I'd ever have thought possible. I had to admire his energy though. He must have been well over seventy yet he could still keep himself awake to shove dog poo through my letter box in the middle of the night and to then keep a bonfire burning all day when the wind was just in the right direction to cover the whole of the garden and house with smoke.

I must admit that I'd had enough last Saturday when I was trying to write the sermon for Sunday's mass. The bishop was coming and I wanted it to be just right for him. All was fine until, about one o'clock in the afternoon, the most horrendous noise came from next door. It was that rap music and it was playing so loudly I couldn't hear myself think. Indeed, it was so loud that the kitchen chairs were moving around by themselves with the vibration.

I knocked on his door but I got no answer. I tried to get on with the sermon but it was impossible. I decided to go and sit in the park where I might at least get some peace and get something done. As I was leaving, I noticed Mr. Ginn at the door with that horrible little dog of his and so I went to have a word with him. I was speechless, however, when I saw that he was actually going into his house! He'd gone out and left that racket playing at full volume on purpose.

He gave me a gloating smile and said, 'Like it, vicar?'

He then went in and turned the music off. I followed him inside. I just had to have a few words with the man. Thankfully he'd let the dog out into the back garden before coming back for another gloat.

'I must say that I can't stand that kind of music myself but then there's no accounting for taste is there?' he said.

God help me Mac but it was the straw that broke the camel's back. I gave it to him right between the eyes. I told him that he was the most odious creature that God had placed upon the earth and that he would try a saint's patience and so on but he just laughed.

'I'm getting to you vicar, aren't I? I thought you religious nutters were all about forgiveness and that. Not going to forgive me then?' he asked sarcastically.'

The priest looked up to heaven before he continued.

'I must admit to you and God that at that point I totally lost it. I called him every name that I could think of. There were an awful lot of Bs, and, may God forgive me, even an F!'

Mac looked at the priest in wonder. He found it hard to even imagine him using such language.

'Go on, Father,' he prompted.

'I suppose that I must have scared him turning on him like that because he rushed off and pulled a shotgun out of a cupboard. He then started brandishing it at me but I had no fear that day. I wrestled with him and I managed to prise the gun out of his hands. I then pointed it right back at him. Seeing the fearful look on his face brought me to my senses and I wondered what on earth I was doing. So, I put the gun in the far corner of the room and left without saying another word.

I hadn't quite closed the front door when I heard the gun go off. I must admit that I froze for a second or two at hearing that terrible sound and I feared that he'd done something terrible. Then I plucked up my courage and went back into the living room and found him lying on the carpet. Half of his face had gone and the gun was on the floor beside him. I was in shock I suppose and, for at least a couple of minutes or so, I must have just stood there in disbelief. Then I finally gathered my wits and phoned the police.

When they came, I told them what had happened and we all assumed that it was suicide. God knows I felt bad enough, I had been tried and I'd failed, failed miserably. I knew that I must have played a big part in that poor man deciding not to go on with his life and committing the grievous sin of suicide. I didn't think it would be possible for me to feel any worse. Dear God, how little did I know then,' he said looking up to the ceiling.

He paused and clasped his hands together as if in prayer.

'I still can't quite believe it but yesterday morning, not long after mass and shamefully in front of some of my parishioners, two policemen came and arrested me. They bundled me into a police car like a common criminal, took me to the police station and charged me with manslaughter.'

'On what grounds?' Mac asked.

'On the grounds that Mr. Ginn couldn't have killed himself as the gun was fired from at least six feet away. It only had two sets of fingerprints on it, mine and Mr. Ginn's. One of Mr. Ginn's neighbours testified that she'd heard the argument and how vicious it had been.

Believe me Mac, I didn't do it but unfortunately all the evidence seems to be saying otherwise,' the priest said giving Mac a look full of desperation.

'I believe you, Father,' Mac said. Then a thought struck him. 'By the way you called the dog horrible, why was that?'

The priest pulled his right trouser leg up and Mac could clearly see the teeth marks.

'It's only a young dog, little more than a puppy I suppose, but that excuse for a human being... no, may God forgive me, I shouldn't be speaking ill of the dead,' the priest said as he made the sign of the cross. 'Anyway, he'd been training the animal to bite anything that moved. I know that even a dog is one of God's creatures and it wasn't the dog's fault but, I'd have to admit that, when he did this to my ankle, I'd have happily thrown it under a bus.'

Mac had to hide a smile.

'Who's handling the case?'

'A big chap called Detective Sergeant Adil Thakkar.'

'Father, leave it with me and try not to worry. I'll get back to you when I know something.'

'Mac, I have to tell you that I can't pay you anything, I have no money.'

'Don't worry about that for a second, Father. After all you've done for me, it's the very least I can do.'

'Thank you, Mac. I prayed that you'd be able to help. Perhaps God is listening after all.'

Mac didn't feel qualified to answer so he just shook Father Pat's hand, smiled and said nothing. The priest left him saying that he was going to go home and have a lie down.

Well, Mac thought, at least Father Pat didn't need to be worried about any loud music coming from next door.

He rang the police station and was pleased that Adil could see him straight away. At the station he followed

27

the sergeant down a corridor. He held the door open and gestured towards a desk in the corner of a large room. It was empty.

The team must be busy with something, Mac thought.

'How's the rugby going?' Mac asked.

Adil smiled. He was a prop forward for the British Police rugby team and he looked every inch the part with his stocky muscular body and tree trunk legs.

'Great, we just thrashed the Air Force a few weeks back. We brought them back down to earth you might say,' Adil said with a smile. His expression then turned to one of concern. 'How are you though, Mac? You had us all worried when you had to be hauled out on a stretcher like that.'

'I'm okay, well better than I was anyway. The rest has definitely done me some good, I'm happy to say.'

'I'm glad of that. Anyway, how can I help you?'

'I'm here on behalf of Father Curran,' Mac said. 'He's a friend of mine and I've told him that I'd try to help him if I could. He's told me a bit about what's happened but I'm not sure that he was making that much sense. I'd be grateful if you could tell me what you're basing your case on.'

'No problem, Mac. Unfortunately for your friend though, it's as clear a case as I've seen. Here, I'll take you through it,' Adil said as he opened the case file on his laptop.

He turned the laptop around so that Mac could see the screen.

'The alarm was raised by two calls Saturday last. One was at thirteen thirty seven, the other just three minutes after that. One of the next-door neighbours, a Mrs. Dellow, was in her back garden and she said that she'd heard a heated argument. Shortly afterwards she heard a gunshot and she called 999 immediately. The other call, logged a few minutes later, was from Father Curran himself.

The ambulance arrived at thirteen forty five and we arrived at thirteen forty nine. When we entered Mr. Ginn's house the paramedics had already declared him dead, not a tough call I suppose as half of his head had gone. Father Curran was in the garden, kind of walking in circles. As I approached him, I could quite clearly hear him say, 'I've killed him, God help me, I've killed him.' However, when he told me his story, about the argument and the struggle for the gun, it seemed a fairly obvious conclusion that Mr. Ginn had killed himself. Then yesterday morning we got the forensics report.

By the spread of buckshot, they calculated that Mr. Ginn was killed from a minimum of six feet away. They were certain that it couldn't have been any nearer so that ruled out suicide. Forensics haven't found any traces that might suggest that someone else could have been in the house so I'm afraid there was only one conclusion we could draw after that. Father Curran shot and killed Albert Ginn.'

'Is there another way that someone could have gotten in? Perhaps from the back of the house?' Mac asked.

'If you like, I'll take you over to the crime scene sometime so that you can see for yourself. Mr. Ginn's house is part of a block of four and, it being one of the two in the centre, there's no side entrance. Apparently there used to be a back entrance into the property but that was permanently blocked off some years ago. The back garden is surrounded by Leylandii and wire fencing on two sides and a sturdy wooden fence on the other side. Mr. Ginn obviously liked his privacy. The fence is well over six feet high and the Leylandii must be nearer twenty. I'll bet that the neighbours must love him for that. Anyway, no-one could have gotten over the two sides that have the Leylandii, they're so close together that they're more or less impenetrable. Not only that but the neighbour from the side that has the fence was in her

29

garden and didn't see anyone climb over. She's the one who first raised the alarm.'

'Is it possible that someone might have hidden in the house?' Mac asked feeling slightly desperate.

'Unfortunately, not. Father Curran himself said he was just about to shut the door behind him when he heard the shot. Then he went back in and saw the body. He said he stood just inside the door for a moment, shocked at the sight I dare say, and that he heard the front door slam shut before he plucked up the courage to go nearer and look at the body. The front door has one of those closer things that shuts the door automatically and pretty vicious it is too. He also says that he sat in the hallway until we arrived as he couldn't bear to be in the same room as the body. So, it appears that no-one could have gotten out of the front of the house.'

Mac sincerely wished that Father Pat has said a little less.

Adil continued, 'We figured that there might have been an outside chance that someone could have been hiding in the house, so we searched it from top to bottom. There was definitely no-one there. I tried the upstairs windows too. They're sash windows. They're old and they've obviously not been opened in years. There must have been at least three or four coats of paint holding them in place. So, that more or less ruled those out as a means of escape. Anyway, we have witnesses who were on the street at the time and they say that they'd have definitely noticed anyone dropping out of a first-floor window. So, I'm afraid that, unless someone could fly over twenty feet high trees, it looks like it has to be Father Curran. I hear that he's a good man, perhaps he's just denying the truth because he can't bear to live with the guilt.'

Mac thought that, unfortunately, this seemed as likely an explanation as any.

30

'When can I get into the house for a look around then?'

'I'm sorry but probably not until Thursday morning now,' Adil replied. 'I've got another case in Stevenage on the go and we've arranged some interviews. They'll take up pretty much all of tomorrow I'm afraid.'

'Thursday morning will be fine,' Mac replied. 'Thanks, Adil.'

He sat in the car for a few minutes wondering what to do next. He knew that there was nothing much he could do for Father Pat until he saw the murder scene so he turned his mind back to Miss Conyers' missing dog.

He fished out the sheet of paper from his pocket and fed Johnny Kinsella's address into his satnav. It was on the outskirts of St. Albans and the satnav told him it would take him forty-five minutes to get there. He stopped at a garage and bought a cold drink and a sandwich to go. He ate the sandwich as he drove while listening to a Vivaldi cello concerto.

He was no classical music buff but he found that the simplicity of Italian baroque music helped to keep him calm at times. As he drove, he wondered what meeting the great Johnny Kinsella would be like. He pictured a massive country mansion, lots of booze and drugs and Johnny surrounded by a horde of minions and skimpily dressed young women arranged around an Olympic-sized swimming pool.

Even with the air conditioning on it was warm inside the car and the thought of sliding into the coolness of a swimming pool was beguiling.

He soon found that he'd been right about the house. He pulled up outside a set of huge wrought iron gates and he could see what looked like a huge stately home on the other side. He pressed the buzzer several times but got no answer. He looked at his watch. It had gone five o'clock and it had been a strange day. He decided to give it another few minutes after which he was going to head back to Letchworth and have a cold and well-earned pint or two in the Magnets. Tim had texted him and told him that he wouldn't get back to Letchworth until late so, for once, he'd be by himself. He was looking forward to it anyway. There he could forget about dogs and priests and actresses for a while.

He got out of the car and noticed that all signs of the earlier rain had gone, already dried up by the early evening's heat. He'd parked in the shade and was sitting on the bonnet of his car, managing to think of nothing in particular, when he was surprised by a man's voice.

'Can I help you mate?' someone asked in a broad Birmingham accent.

Mac turned to see a man standing behind him holding a plastic carrier bag. He had long hair and was dressed simply in ripped jeans and a plain black tee shirt. It had almost been a lifetime since he'd seen him last and Mac was surprised that he hadn't changed all that much. The long hair had streaks of grey in it and his face was a little more lined but it was unmistakeably him.

The king of heavy metal himself, Johnny Kinsella.

Chapter Five

'You're not a fan, are you?' Johnny asked with a worried expression as he took a defensive step backwards.

'No, you're absolutely safe there,' Mac replied.

He fished a card out of his pocket and gave it to Johnny.

Johnny smiled broadly, 'I'm glad that you're not a fan, I'm trying to keep this place a secret.'

He read the card.

'Bloody hell, I've never met a proper private detective before.' He suddenly became defensive again. 'This isn't about paternity or anything like that, is it? Some of these young girls must think I can make them pregnant just by looking at them.'

'No, I'm representing Cathy Conyers,' Mac said.

'Cathy? Bloody hell, you'd better come in then,' Johnny said with a frown.

He opened a little side gate and led Mac towards the house.

'Are you alright walking, with that crutch and all?' Johnny asked.

Mac assured him that he'd be fine while thinking that it was nice to be asked. Most people just tried to ignore the crutch and his limp as if mentioning it might remind him that he was disabled. His pain never let him forget that fact.

Rather than heading to the huge front door Johnny took him around the side of the house to what, presumably, would have been the tradesmen's entrance in years gone by. Johnny then led him down a short hallway and he found himself in a truly remarkable kitchen. It was remarkable because, in so grand a house, it was quite ordinary and looked much like the one Mac had at home. Johnny placed his bag on a work surface and got out a plastic bottle of milk, a loaf of bread and some butter.

'Just fancied a slice of toast for some reason and there's a nice little shop just down the road. It reminds me of what shops used to be like when I was a kid. Fancy a cup of tea?'

'Yes, please and a slice of toast too would be nice if you've got any going spare,' Mac said still feeling a little hungry.

They took their tea and toast into the room next door. It was about the size of Mac's living room and it had a neatly made single bed in the corner. Several guitars were strewn around the room, one of which was plugged into a small amplifier. On a table by the far window there was a laptop that was hooked up to the biggest monitor screen that Mac had ever seen. Nearby there was an electronic keyboard and a microphone on a stand. Mac and Johnny sat on a small sofa that had seen better days.

Johnny saw Mac looking at the laptop.

'You know, years ago you had to have these great big tape machines and a mixer desk with a zillion control knobs and faders to record anything decent. All you need is a computer now.'

'You live in this room?' Mac asked in some surprise.

'Yes, it was only supposed to be for a few days while I got things sorted out after Cathy kicked me out but I sort of got stuck here. Anyway, I've lived in far worse, believe me. I picked this room because it's small and near the kitchen. I suppose it was used by the servants for something or other when the house was in its glory days. The rest of the rooms are far too big for me, as is the whole house if I'm being honest. It's like some bloody great spooky mausoleum and it gives me the willies at times.'

'So, why did you buy it then?' Mac asked.

'My accountant said that it would be a good investment. We had someone who lived in and looked after the place but, when me and Cathy split up, I decided to move in myself. For some reason I didn't want to be too far away from her.' Johnny gave Mac a strained smile. 'Anyway, I think I can detect a bit of a Brummie accent. Where are you from exactly?'

'Small Heath.'

'Really? I used to work in a music shop in Small Heath when I was young. God but I loved that job. All I had to do was serve a few customers and then play guitar for the rest of the day. I come from Stechford, just a few bus stops down the road from Small Heath. You know we used to live in a two up, two down, six of us would you believe, and it never seemed crowded to me. I loved that house but as I said this place just gives me the willies. There's just too much of it and I'm sure we've got some ghosts here as well,' Johnny confided in a low voice. 'You get a lot of funny noises at night sometimes.'

There was silence for a moment and then Johnny said with a sigh, 'Okay, I suppose you'd better let me know what Cathy wants. She's had the bloody house and the dog so what does she want now?'

'She wants the dog.'

Johnny looked puzzled.

'She's got the dog, hasn't she?'

Mac shook his head.

'The dog's been missing for two days now and she's convinced that you've got it.'

It was now Johnny's turn to shake his head.

'No bloody way! I must admit that I've thought of dognapping Sharmy a few times but I know what Cathy's like. She'd have a gang of lawyers on me and they'd have the kegs off me arse in no time. Poor Sharmy though, I hope she's alright.'

'What were you doing in the house last Friday? The chauffeur said that he saw you there with a dog lead,' Mac asked.

'It was just me being stupid as usual. I was missing Sharmy, I suppose, and I thought that it wouldn't do any harm to take her for a walk. I looked around but I couldn't find her.'

'So, you haven't got the dog?' Mac asked.

'No, I wish I had. I could do with the company to be honest,' Johnny said with a mournful expression.

'Do you mind if I have a look around?'

'Help yourself.'

Mac looked around the kitchen first. He opened all the cupboards but there was no sign of a dog bowl or cans of dog food. He looked outside but there was no water bowl, no kennel and no sign of a dog. He went through a couple of the nearby rooms. His steps echoed in their emptiness and the shadows took on sinister shapes. He could understand how Johnny felt about the house, it was far too large and he felt small and lonely as he wandered around the empty rooms.

In a house this size a dog could be hidden anywhere so he decided to give up and take Johnny's word for it.

Mac could hear a guitar playing as he walked back. Johnny was playing an improvisation around an old blues riff and doing it really well too. He then heard Johnny sing...

'When I was a young boy, around the age of five, my mother said I was gonna be the greatest man alive...'

Mac stood outside the door listening avidly. He had to stop himself from joining in the chorus, 'I'm a man, I'm a full-grown man...'

Johnny stopped when he entered the room.

'Satisfied that Sharmy's not here?'

Mac nodded.

'I wish you hadn't stopped playing though. I was really enjoying that.'

36

'I can't believe that you're a Muddy Waters fan too. How did you get into blues music?' Johnny asked.

'Well, many years ago a good friend of mine took me to a place called Charlie's Blues House. It sounded exotic but it was just an upstairs room in a rundown city centre pub in Birmingham.'

'Bloody hell, you used to go to Charlie's!' Johnny exclaimed in surprise.

'I used to like the Stones, Van Morrison, even Fleetwood Mac before they went all pop, but I'd never listened to real blues music before. So, that night a young local band did the first set and they were okay, a reasonable racket. Then, while the second band were getting their gear set up, they played some blues tracks over the PA. That's when it happened. This particular track started with a riff, kind of a walking pace and then this sound hit me between the eyes and the hair on my neck stood up...'

'Let me guess. Howling Wolf, Smokestack Lightning,' Johnny said excitedly.

'You've got it. I must have been in some sort of trance as I listened to it. I'd never heard anything remotely like it before but then I was suddenly brought back to reality with a horrible thud.'

'What happened?'

'Your band started playing,' Mac said drolly.

Johnny laughed so much that Mac thought he was going to fall off the sofa.

'Yes, we were bloody rough in those days,' he said with a huge smile.

'Anyway, after that I started hunting down as many blues albums as I could and I've never stopped listening to them since. Well not until fairly recently anyway.'

'Why what happened?' Johnny asked.

Mac could see from Johnny's face that he was really interested and he found that he was beginning to like Johnny Kinsella. There was something open and honest about him that he'd never have expected to have found in a famous rock star.

'My wife died. I haven't listened to anything much since except a bit of classical now and again.'

'I'm sorry to hear about your wife. God, that must have been bloody rough. I'm only divorced from mine and that hurts enough. I don't know what it would be like if she...' Johnny left the sentence unfinished. 'Anyway, what classical stuff do you like?'

'Italian baroque, you know...'

'Yeah, Vivaldi, Albinoni, Corelli. I quite like that myself. Have you tried Lully or Purcell yet?'

Mac shook his head.

'You should, especially Purcell. I sometimes put him on when I'm writing lyrics believe it or not.'

Johnny had surprised him again. As Johnny seemed to be so open Mac thought he might as well ask.

'Johnny, I have to admit that you're quite different to what I imagined but can I ask...?'

'It's about the snakes I'll bet, that's what everyone wants to know about. Am I right?'

Mac nodded.

'I've never told anyone outside of the band this before but, as you're a fellow Brummie, and if you promise to keep it under your hat...' Johnny said as he looked left and then right.

Mac promised faithfully.

'Okay, one of our most popular songs at our gigs is called Rattlesnake. That's why we have snakes on the band's logos and such. Well, one night many years ago I'm bashing it out when this snake comes flying out of the side of the stage and hits me right on the head. It looked so bloody realistic that I was sure it was a real snake. It was just pure reaction that made me catch it before it hit the floor. Anyway, I could tell immediately by the feel of it that it was a fake and then I look over and there's my manager standing in the wings and he's killing himself laughing. So, I shook the snake, to make it look like it was alive and trying to get out of my grasp, and then I thought, I'll show him. I then bit the head off the plastic snake and spat it back at him. Well, the whole place went totally apeshit. Afterwards fans swore that they'd seen me bite the head off a king cobra, some said it was two snakes, some said as many as six snakes. You just can't underestimate the power of the urban myth. So, on seeing the crowd's reaction, my manager picked up the two bits of the plastic snake and locked them away in the boot of his car. Then, afterwards at the press conference, he doesn't quite say it but he kind of implies that I'm a total nutter who is now biting the heads off snakes and God only knows what I might get up to during the next gig. After that ticket sales went through the roof for the rest of the tour and we've never looked back. Life can be really funny sometimes, can't it?'

'Thanks for telling me that and don't worry. I won't tell a soul that in real life Johnny Kinsella is actually quite a nice bloke and spoil your image.' Mac stood up, 'So, that's it then. I'll take your word that you haven't got the dog and I'll report back accordingly.'

'Thanks, and give my best to Cathy. Tell her...well, just tell her that I'm here.'

'Can you do me a favour?' Mac produced the sheet of paper with Johnny's address on and gave him the blank side. 'Can I have your autograph? It's for my friend Tim. He's a fellow Brummie too and a massive fan of yours.'

'Sure, say why don't you and Tim come over some time?' Johnny suggested. 'We could have a few beers, play some music and talk about the old days. I'd really like that.'

Mac could only ask which day. He knew that Tim would be absolutely over the moon.

'Well, tomorrow night we've got a one-off charity gig with some other bands at the Albert Hall, but otherwise

I'm here for the next three weeks trying to write some material for the new album. So, anytime really. After that I have to move out and then it's back to Brum for rehearsals with the band.'

Johnny added his mobile number to the sheet of paper.

'Thanks, Johnny,' Mac said and they shook hands.

'Arley-barley, wait a minute. As you're coming back...' Johnny disappeared and came back a few minutes later with an old vinyl LP. 'Here, you can lend this for a bit if you like.'

Mac looked at the cover. It had a line drawing of a wolf howling at a full moon. He could feel his heartbeat running faster.

'Is this the original fifty-nine album?'

'Yeah, even better though, pull out the record,' Johnny said.

Mac reverentially pulled out the vinyl disc. On the paper cover was written 'To Graham, thanks for everything, Chester'.

Mac was stunned. He ran his fingers lightly over the writing.

'Signed by the Wolf himself, Chester Burnett. How did you come by this?'

'Sit down for a minute and I'll tell you,' Johnny said.

Mac sat down clutching the precious disc to his chest.

'My manager, the snake thrower, is the Graham in the dedication. In sixty-five he was only twenty or so and he was desperate to be involved in the music scene. As the poor sod can't sing and is totally tone deaf, the only thing he could do was get involved in managing acts and putting together tours and so on. Anyway, because he's so bloody good at it, he got to be a big name in the business pretty quickly. He'd been hearing about this Howling Wolf, I mean the Stones, the Animals, the Yardbirds, all the bands were doing covers of his stuff. So, Graham says to himself, I'm going to bring him over to England and he did and to the Marquee in London no less.

So, the Wolf, for all that he was six and half feet tall and built like a brick shithouse, was a bit nervous. He actually asked Graham if he was sure that people would come to the gig. He didn't think it possible that anyone in a country so far away would know about his music. So, when he went on stage and looked around the room, he was amazed to see members of some of the top bands in the world sitting in the audience and they'd come just to see him. Graham said that he'd never heard anything like it, before or since. He said Wolf wasn't just a performer but a force of nature and more than a bit scary with it too. At the end of the night the audience were howling too and they wouldn't let him leave the stage and don't forget that, as I said, this audience were composed of some of the best musicians of their time. So, when we have a great gig and get a bit big headed, Graham always says, 'That was really great but it wasn't Wolf.' God, I'd have loved to seen him live on stage but he died in seventy-six.'

'Me too,' Mac said, 'Thanks again, Johnny, for the record and for the story.'

As he drove home, Mac wondered again about how your preconceived ideas about people can turn out to be so wrong. Johnny, the proclaimed bad boy of heavy metal, was just a straight forward man who seemed to have been left pretty much untouched by the years of fame. He remembered his mother used to say to him, 'Money can't buy the really important things in life.' Johnny seemed to be an object lesson in this.

He could probably afford to buy half of Hertfordshire but all his money couldn't stop him from being lonely.

Chapter Six

Early that Wednesday morning a gnawing pain woke him just as dawn was breaking. He needed to go to the toilet and so, with some trepidation, he stood up. He wasn't totally surprised when a wave of pain like a bolt of white lightning ran down his left leg. It made him catch his breath and it was so intense that he nearly blacked out. He'd been warned by the doctors that he might have pain episodes like this. He'd gotten away with it so far and so he was quite unprepared for the intensity of the attack.

Mac grabbed his phone and was about to call Amrit when he remembered that she wasn't going to be around today. She was going to the Science Museum in London for a day out with her youngest son. He knew that she'd come if he phoned her but she'd been so looking forward to her little trip that Mac didn't have the heart to spoil it for her. His daughter Bridget and her boyfriend Tommy were, of course, thousands of miles away on holiday and hopefully enjoying the Mediterranean sunshine.

He sighed. He could always ring his friend Tim but what would be the point? Apart from Amrit and her magical acupuncture needles there was really no point in involving anyone else.

After the intensity had lessened a little it was replaced by a grinding pain in his lower back that he knew from experience could not be argued with and would not quickly go away. He stumbled to the toilet, thankfully only a few steps away from his bedroom, and winced at every step as he made his way back to the bedroom.

He always kept some medication and a bottle of water near his bed just in case. He put a fresh Fentanyl patch on to dull the pain and then decided to take what he called the nuclear option. This consisted of two small round blue pills. They were a type of pain killer too but, fortunately for Mac, they also had the side effect of knocking him out cold for a minimum of twelve hours. He yelped as the pain hit him again as he got back into bed. He lay on his back praying that unconsciousness would arrive as soon as possible.

It took what seemed like an eternity but eventually Mac gratefully slipped into oblivion.

The pills did their work and he awoke at seven in the evening. He gingerly tried to stand up and he was relieved that the pain was once again back to being just about bearable. He made himself a scratch meal of beans on toast and then replayed the messages on his answer-phone. There were three in all, two from Father Curran asking if he'd made any progress in his case and one from Tim inviting him to the pub. Mac found that didn't even have the energy to return the calls. He suddenly felt desperately tired and stumbled back to his bed.

He awoke early Thursday morning and wondered where his Wednesday had gone. However, the long sleep had refreshed him and the pain had eased off a little more. After a shower and a shave, he felt ready to take on the world. He wanted to be there in plenty of time for his appointment with Adil but, before he left the house, he took the time to unlock the cupboard and check that the Howling Wolf album was still there.

Satisfied that it was real and that it hadn't been stolen in the night, he locked the cupboard again. Before he left the house, he carefully checked that all the windows and doors were locked too, just in case. As he drove to his appointment Mac couldn't help thinking how surprised and pleased his friend Tim would be when he finally got to tell him about his meeting with Johnny Kinsella.

Adil was waiting for him when he pulled up outside Albert Ginn's house. Mac glanced at the house. It was the left of the two centre houses, a sturdy house with a peaked roof and, quite typically for Letchworth, rendered white. It hadn't been repainted for a while and the white was now more of a shade of yellow.

'Good morning, Mac,' Adil said holding out his hand.

Mac shook his hand.

'Ready for the tour?' Adil asked.

'I certainly am and thanks for doing this.'

Adil led the way to the front door which was set behind a small front garden that had seen better days. The door itself was old and quite beautiful, Mac thought, with its stained-glass segments gleaming in the morning sunlight. His wife would have known whether it was Arts and Crafts or Art Nouveau but Mac didn't have a clue. He just knew that he liked it.

Adil pulled a bunch of keys from his pocket and opened the door. Mac stepped inside. It had been a while since the house had been redecorated and it was looking a bit faded and shabby now. However, he could also see that it must have been a fine house in its time. He turned as Adil entered behind him and watched the door close quickly by itself. Adil had had been right about the door closer. It worked all too efficiently.

'So, this was where your client sat while he waited for us,' Adil said as he pointed to a chair that stood on the left of the wide hallway.

He led Mac through another door and into the living room. He didn't need to show Mac where the body had lain as the brown carpet was matted with blood.

'So, where was Mr. Ginn standing when he was shot?' Mac asked.

'Just about here we think,' Adil replied standing in the middle of the room and turned slightly towards the French doors at the other end of the room.

'And where was the killer standing?'

Adil went over towards the French doors and turned around.

44

'Just about here somewhere they think. It's six feet away from the body and you can see some of the buckshot in the wall opposite.'

'I take it that the doors were open?' Mac asked.

'Yes, Father Curran said that Mr. Ginn had let his dog out into the garden before they started speaking. It was a hot day so it was no surprise that he left the doors open.'

'And I take it that's why the next-door neighbour could hear them arguing so clearly?'

'Yes, she seems to have heard every word,' Adil said. 'Her story of what was said tallies more or less exactly with that of Father Curran's.'

'Can we have a look around the garden?' Mac asked.

Adil took out the bunch of keys again and opened the double doors. The garden beyond was larger than Mac had expected, a long rectangular expanse of grass with bushes and flowers around the edges. He stepped out and stood on the lawn. His heart sunk as he looked around him.

The garden was the same width as the house and, as Adil had said, there were no side entrances. The bottom and the right-hand side of the garden were bordered by tightly packed rows of extremely tall Leylandii trees. At the foot of the trees there ran a wire link fence that was some five feet high. On the left-hand side a long, solid looking wooden fence ran the complete length of the garden. Mac walked around all three sides. The Leylandii trees had grown so tightly packed together that they looked impenetrable even without the wire fence which Mac supposed was for the benefit of the dog. He examined the wire fence along its entire length anyway. If anyone was in a hurry and had tried to climb over there should have been some sort of damage or warping of the fence. There was nothing.

He next examined the long wooden fence which, unfortunately, seemed in very good repair. Mac sighed.

45

It wasn't made up of flimsy panels like so many others he'd seen. The wooden planks making up the fence were over an inch thick and stood well over six feet in height. Mac commented on its solidity.

'Anyway, even if the fencing hadn't been as solid as it is, the next-door neighbour was in the garden at the time. She'd have seen anyone trying to escape that way,' Adil helpfully pointed out.

Mac was still trying to believe that Father Pat was as innocent as he claimed but he was finding it increasingly difficult.

'Would it be okay if we had a quick word with the neighbour?' Mac asked.

'Sure, so long as it's okay with her,' Adil replied. 'Let's go and see if she's in.'

As they opened the gate to go into next door's front garden, they couldn't help noticing that a large 'For Sale' sign had been erected. Mac looked up and down the street and could see at least half a dozen houses nearby with the same signs.

'They weren't up Tuesday,' Adil said. 'All of a sudden it seems like people can't wait to get away from here.'

Remembering what Father Pat had said about his neighbour being a 'one-man blight' on the local housing market, Mac didn't think that this was a co-incidence. Looking at the number of signs, Mac thought that there might be no lack of people who had a motive for doing away with Albert Ginn.

Mrs. Dellow was in and she was happy to talk to them. She must have been in her late sixties, white haired, her face crinkled with a permanent smile. She looked just like everyone's favourite granny should.

'I see that you're selling up?' Mac asked.

'Oh yes, I couldn't bear to live here now, not after...' she let the sentence hang.

'Have you had much interest?'

'Oh yes, I only contacted the estate agents a couple of days ago and I'm letting it go at a good price. Believe it or not I've already had an offer, cash too. I'm hoping to sign the papers soon,' she replied with a wide smile.

'I know that you've already told the police what happened but I'd be grateful if you could tell it once again,' Mac said.

'Oh, that's no problem dear, I'm always up for a little chat. Where shall I start from then?'

'If you start from where you heard the two men arguing,' Mac prompted.

'I was out in the garden with my secateurs tidying up some rose bushes when I heard Albert open up the French windows. It was only then that I heard the raised voices. I recognised them immediately and I was really surprised at some of the language that came from Father Curran. It wasn't exactly what you'd expect to hear from a man of the cloth, I must say. Anyway, it went quiet for a few moments then I heard a deafening blast and I knew it was from a shotgun. My father used to shoot, you see, and so I'm quite familiar with the sound. So, fearing the worst, I phoned the police straight away.'

'What do you mean by 'fearing the worst'?' Mac asked.

'Well, I knew that Albert owned a shotgun and that he sometimes kept it loaded, in case of foxes he said. He really didn't like foxes in his garden for some reason. I told him that it was dangerous and that he could get into trouble letting off a shotgun but he wouldn't listen to sense. Anyway, when I heard the gun go off, I thought that Albert had shot Father Curran. I was quite surprised when I found out that it was the other way around.'

'You call him 'Albert'. Were you and Mr. Ginn friends?' Mac asked.

'Yes, not close friends, but I'd say we were friendly. I've lived next door to Albert for over forty years. He and my late husband were cousins and best friends since childhood. I know that he wasn't all that popular with other people but Albert and I got on alright.'

Mac turned as he heard a growling from behind him. A small Jack Russell terrier stood baring its teeth at him.

'Go to bed Terry, right now,' Mrs. Dellow ordered.

The dog reluctantly retreated into the kitchen.

'Is that Mr. Ginn's dog?' Mac asked.

'Yes, the police have been very good and said I could look after him.'

'Terry's an unusual name for a dog. Do you know why he called him that?' Mac asked.

'Oh, all of Albert's dogs have been called Terry,' she replied. 'He was mad about Terry Wogan. He never missed one of his shows on the radio.'

'So, how are you finding him?' Mac asked.

'You have to make sure that you're firm with him but he's a very nice little dog really.'

Mac, remembering the teeth marks on Father Pat's ankle, was still somewhat doubtful about this and kept glancing at the kitchen door in case the dog managed to sneak back in.

'Anyway, did you notice anything else unusual around the time of the shooting?' Mac asked desperately fishing for anything that might help his client.

She gave it some thought and then said, 'Sorry, no. Until I heard the argument it had been a perfectly normal day.'

She offered them both a cup of tea but, when they declined, she let them go with the sweetest of smiles.

'I wouldn't like to have her giving evidence against me,' Adil said.

'Yes, I know what you mean. You'd have to be churlish not to believe such a nice little old lady.'

Adil's phone rang. He said 'yes' a couple of times, wrote down an address and then said with some excitement, 'Okay, I'm on my way. I should be there in about half an hour.'

'I take it that you have to run then?' Mac asked.

'Yes, there's been a robbery near Shaw's Corner and she's famous too...'

'Miss Cathy Conyers by any chance?' Mac asked.

'How on earth could you have known that?' Adil asked giving Mac a look of baffled respect.

'I've been doing some work for her.' Mac was loath to explain exactly what. 'I might be able to help you with this one. Do you mind if I tag along?'

'That's fine with me and I'm sure Dan would love to see you anyway.'

Adil drove quite fast down the country lanes and Mac found it hard to keep up with him. The electric gates were wide open when they arrived. Mac saw four men enter the front door wearing all-in-one plastic suits with hoods. If they needed that many of the forensics team to process the scene then Mac knew that it had to be more than a simple robbery.

A tall, sandy haired man stood outside the front door looking inside. Mac smiled.

'Andy, how are you?' Mac said as he came nearer.

DI Reid turned and smiled broadly too.

'Mac, it's great to see you're up and about again. How's your back?'

They shook hands vigorously.

'Not so bad. I'm working anyway and that helps a bit.'

'You know I remember once when you came back to work after breaking your arm, it was the Maxwell case if I remember right, and we were all surprised. But you just said that 'Work is the best painkiller' and carried on regardless.'

Mac smiled at the memory. Andy had been part of his team when he'd been in charge of the London murder squad.

Just history now, he thought with some sadness.

'Yes, but it wasn't the pain that was the worst thing about that. I remember that I had an itch in a spot under

49

the plaster that I couldn't quite reach, not even with a knitting needle. It nearly drove me doolally that did. Anyway, where's Dan?' Mac asked.

'He's inside talking to the forensics team,' Andy said motioning him to look inside the front door.

He went over to the front door. He could see right inside the same living room where, not long ago, he'd sat and talked to Cathy Conyers. He could also see the reason why the forensics team were called in.

A body lay on its side in the centre of the room, a fan of blood around the head staining the light-coloured carpet. The left-hand side of the head had been reduced to a pulp but Mac still recognised him straight away.

It was Ben Meeks, the actress's chauffeur, who was lying on the floor with the side of his head smashed in.

Chapter Seven

Dan Carter came out looking as rumpled and unshaven as ever. He was looking thoughtful but his face broke into a smile when he saw Mac.

'You must be telepathic or something. I was just thinking of calling you and now you turn up. How are you, Mac?' Dan asked as they shook hands.

'I'm fine. Have you identified the body yet?'

'No, I rang Miss Conyers and told her that there'd been a break-in that's all. I didn't want to tell her that there'd been a murder over the phone. She'll be on her way back here shortly. I was hoping that she'll be able to ID the body when she gets here.'

'Well, I can save you some time then. The body in there belongs to Ben Meeks.'

Dan flashed Mac a look of astonishment.

'How on earth could you know that?'

'I've met him before. He's Miss Conyers' chauffeur,' Mac replied.

'The chauffeur? Tell me how you know him then,' Dan said.

Mac raised his eyes to heaven. He knew he'd have to come clean and tell them that he'd been employed as a dog catcher. He wasn't looking forward to it.

After he'd finished Dan was smiling when he asked, 'So, you never did find the dog?'

Mac shook his head.

Wanting to change the subject he continued, 'You said that there'd been a robbery. Was it the painting?'

'I don't know anything about a painting but there's a gap on one of the walls and it's the only thing that's obviously missing so far. This painting, was it worth much do you know?' Dan asked.

'I should say so. It's by the Norwegian painter Edvard Munch. One of his more famous paintings, The Scream,

51

sold for nearly a hundred and twenty million dollars recently. I looked it up on the internet. Miss Conyers' little painting probably wouldn't get that much but I'm pretty sure it would still be worth tens of millions.'

Dan raised his eyebrows.

'And she kept the original here, not a copy?'

'That's what she told me,' Mac replied.

'Do you think that maybe the chauffeur tried to stop the thieves and that's how he ended up dead?' Andy surmised.

'Could be,' Mac replied. 'Only he and the cook lived in the house beside Miss Conyers as far as I know. I think there's a gardener too but I'm fairly sure he only came in during the day. Where is the cook by the way?'

'At her sick sister's in Cambridge or so I've been told,' Dan replied.

'So, how was Miss Conyers when you spoke to her?'

'Well, she was upset enough about the break in, so God knows what she going to be like when she finds out that she's going to have to get a new chauffeur,' Dan said. 'Apparently, she was supposed to have been filming in Manchester today. She only arrived there last night.'

Mac was thoughtful for a moment.

'Strange isn't it, that the thieves should pick the one night that the cook's away and also when there was no dog to bother them?'

'So, you think that the dog's disappearance might not be a coincidence then?' Dan asked.

'We all know burglars hate dogs, especially big dogs. They're totally unpredictable so it's best if you can remove such unpredictability if you can, but how? The dog could have escaped when the gate was left open for a short time recently but that would have been just leaving things to chance. I think someone got rid of the dog and, as the place is such a bloody fortress, I think it was most likely someone from inside the house.'

'So, that would give us just three suspects, the cook, the gardener and the chauffeur,' Dan said

'Four. Let's not forget Miss Conyers herself,' Mac replied. 'People have been known to rob their own houses before. No five, her ex-husband, Johnny Kinsella, still had access to the property.'

'It's not likely that it would be either of those though, is it? And why get rid of the dog in that case?' Dan thought for a moment and answered his own question. 'Unless it was to make us think that someone else was responsible. Yes, people have done it for the insurance money before so we'd better check just to be sure.' Dan turned to Andy and Adil. 'Andy, can you track down Johnny Kinsella and see what he knows? Adil, call in and ask Martin if we can get a court order for Miss Conyers' financial records and see what we can dig up there. Let's see if she's got any money worries.'

'Where does this Johnny Kinsella live?' Andy asked.

Mac gave him the address.

'I'm not sure he'll be there though. He said that he was playing at the Albert Hall last night.'

Andy took his phone out and got onto the internet. After a few minutes on Google he frowned and passed the phone to Mac. It was a tabloid paper's website and it showed a picture of Johnny Kinsella leaving a party in London just after two in the morning. A startlingly beautiful young girl had an arm draped around his neck. He passed the phone to Dan.

'I remember when I was young my mother kept telling me to stop wasting my time playing the guitar as it would never get me anywhere in life,' Dan said wistfully.

'I suppose that rules him out then,' Andy commented.

'It depends on when Ben was killed. Anyway, I suppose he could have paid someone to do it,' Dan said sounding unconvinced by his own words.

Mac gave Andy Johnny's mobile number. He wasn't surprised when he heard Andy having to leave a message.

'So, what about the cook and the gardener?' Mac asked.

'The cook is on her way here. The Cambridge police are giving her a lift as she doesn't drive,' Dan said. 'As for the gardener, who should have reported for work by now, all I've got is a name and address.'

He passed a sheet of paper to Mac. The gardener's name was James Stourton and he lived in Welwyn Garden City, somewhere on the Broadwater Estate.

'By the way who called it in?' Mac asked.

'An anonymous male caller,' Dan said. 'As it was a murder report, the uniforms checked it out straight away. They found the front gate wide open and the body in the living room.'

Dan glanced over at Adil who was still on the phone. 'When he's finished fancy coming with us to Welwyn? The forensics team won't let us near the place for a while so we might as well be doing something. Andy, can you hold the fort here? If you hear from Johnny Kinsella let me know.'

Mac was more than happy to accept the offer. As they drove down the road, he saw a sign for Welwyn Garden City and it reminded him of something else Ben had said.

'I nearly forgot but there's also someone else we should also consider.'

'Who's that?' Dan asked.

'Eleanor Tarbridge,' Mac replied. 'She's Miss Conyers' personal assistant and they're very close apparently.'

'So, where's she now, with Miss Conyers?'

'No, she's somewhere in the Caribbean at the moment, she's on a cruise with her husband. She's been on it since before the break-in.'

'So, it's not likely to be her then, is it?' Dan said.

'Who knows? It's certainly a good alibi though. And it's something of a coincidence with her, Miss Conyers, the cook and the dog all being out of the way at the same time, isn't it?'

He could see Dan mentally file the thought away for the future.

The gardener's address turned out to be a second floor flat in a nondescript and slightly run-down housing estate just off the Broadwater Road. They rang the bell several times but no-one came to the door. Dan then rang next door's bell and a middle-aged man in a pair of faded pyjamas opened the door. Adil flashed his warrant card and the man reluctantly held the door open for them. Mac could hear the Radio Four news in the background. When they entered the living room the man made no move to turn the radio off.

'And your name is?' Dan asked.

'Ronald Snaithe,' the man replied looking worried.

'This is nothing to do with you Mr. Snaithe. I'm interested in Mr. James Stourton. Can you tell me anything about him?'

The man sat down in the only seat in the room, an armchair that had seen better days. Looking around Mac concluded that the whole flat had seen better days.

'James Stourton? Who's he?' Mr. Snaithe asked.

'The man who lives next door,' Dan replied.

'Oh, him. I never knew that was his name. He seemed okay, always said hello on the few occasions we met on the landing. It was the only place I met him though. I don't get out much, the legs aren't up to much these days,' he said looking immensely sorry for himself.

'He doesn't seem to be at home. Have you any idea where he might be?'

'Oh, they've gone. I'm afraid you've missed them. They left a couple of hours ago.'

'What do you mean, gone? And who is 'they'?' Dan asked.

'I didn't sleep well so I was up early this morning. I was listening to the radio when I heard him leaving for work.' Mr. Snaithe stopped and gave it some deep thought. 'Yes, that's right, 'Tweet of the Day' was on so it was just before the six o'clock news. It was bramblings today, something else I've learnt about. Anyway, where was I?'

'Mr. Stourton left at six,' Dan prompted.

'Oh yes. I was surprised when I heard him running up the stairs again just before seven. I thought that he must have forgotten something. Then, half an hour later, I saw them put some suitcases in his van and they left.'

'They?' Dan prompted.

'Yes, Mr. Stourton and his wife and their baby,' Mr. Snaithe said.

'What did the van look like?'

'It was fairly big, white, just a van really.'

They thanked Mr. Snaithe and left him to his radio.

'It looks like the gardener might be putting himself in the frame,' Adil commented.

'You're right there,' Mac replied. 'I wonder if they've established the time of Ben Meeks' death yet?'

'Well, let's get back and see what forensics can tell us. With any luck the cook should be there by now as well,' Dan said.

The gate was shut when they got back to the house. Andy pulled it open to let them in.

'I'm sorry, I was just trying to make it look as normal as possible. Luckily, this road doesn't get much traffic so I don't think that anyone's twigged as yet.'

'Let's keep it like that for as long as possible. Have forensics found anything yet?' Dan said nodding towards the house.

'No, I asked a few minutes ago. They said that there's nothing new so far but it's still early days,' Andy replied.

Dan turned to Adil and said, 'Can you have a scout around and see if you can find somewhere nearby that we could use as an incident room? I want to get the rest of the team involved as soon as possible.'

Adil nodded and set off on his quest.

Dan then turned back to Mac and Andy and mournfully shook his head.

'So, we have a murder case involving a soap actress and a rock star. They're not exactly who I would have chosen to be involved in a murder case. God, the press are so going to be all over this one when they find out! I really hate it when they start sticking their noses into everything.'

Mac knew what he meant. He'd had more than a few cases in the past where press interference had made life really difficult. He remembered one in particular where a story in a tabloid had actually tipped off a murderer that they were on to him. He'd gotten away and managed to kill again before Mac's team had finally cornered him.

'And, if that isn't enough of a problem, I'm going to be shorthanded before long as well,' Dan continued looking even more glum than usual. 'Jo and Gerry are getting married in a couple of weeks and I can hardly ask them to postpone that.'

Mac was nearly forgetting about the wedding. If the investigation was still ongoing by then poor Jo and Gerry might find that half of their guests wouldn't be able to make it.

'By the way the cook's arrived,' Andy said as he pointed towards a police car.

Dan turned around and saw a middle-aged woman sitting patiently in a car on the driveway. They went over to her.

She told them that her name was Alice Rodgers. Andy checked with forensics first before she led them around the side of the house and opened the door to a little annex which contained the kitchen. They all sat around a huge table and Alice insisted on making everyone a cup of tea before being interviewed. Mac thought that she seemed like a pleasant woman and fitted the stereotype of a cook being middle-aged and comfortably padded.

'I just can't believe that Ben's dead,' she said, shaking her head as she said the words. 'I was only speaking to him yesterday. I remember I said that I needed more flour for the scones and he was about to pop out and get me some when I got the phone call about my sister. She's never been strong, God help her, and when I heard that she'd been involved in an accident...'

'An accident?' Dan asked. 'I thought that she was just ill.'

'No dear, she has one of those little electric gadabouts that people seem to be using everywhere now. She was on her way to the shops when a car hit her while she was crossing the road.'

'How is she?'

'She's not too bad actually, shaken more than anything,' the cook replied. 'The car didn't hit her too hard, just enough to turn her little gadabout over. I told her off for being a ninny but she said that it wasn't her fault. The car had stopped for her but once she started crossing the road the car jerked forward and hit her. She thought that his foot must have slipped off the brake.'

'That was very convenient,' Dan said softly.

'Sorry, what was that dear?' Alice asked.

'Oh, nothing. What did the car do then?'

'He drove off without a backward glance, so she said. Unfortunately, there are some heartless people in this world.'

'You say 'he', did your sister get a look at the driver then?' Dan asked.

'Sorry no, she didn't. Her eyesight's not all that good anyway, poor dear. She told the police it was a 'he' but, when they asked her the same question, she said that it was quite possible that it could have been a woman,' she replied.

'And the car? Did she get a look at that?' Dan persisted.

'Yes, she was very specific about that. She said that it was definitely black,' Alice said.

'It was black,' Dan repeated. 'Did she have idea of the make of car or registration?'

'Oh no dear, she wouldn't have a clue about anything like that.'

Dan decided to give up on that line of questioning.

'Did Ben hear you when you were on the phone to your sister?'

'Yes, he must have. Anyway, I told him all about it so he could tell Miss Conyers in case I needed to be in Cambridge for a few days. Poor chap.'

'Has anything unusual happened in the last week or so?' Mac asked.

Alice gave this some thought before finally saying, 'No, apart from that lovely dog disappearing like that. Miss Conyers was really upset about it. I think that she was even more upset that Eleanor wasn't around to console her. She needed a shoulder to cry on, the poor dear.'

'What about you and Ben?' Mac asked.

'Oh, she was very good to the both of us but she would never ask that of us. It was only Johnny and Eleanor that she confided in and, after Johnny left, it was just Eleanor.'

Mac had got the impression that Cathy Conyers was made of sterner stuff but from what the cook said it appears that he might have been wrong. Mac wondered if she was mostly front after all.

'By the way have you got a picture of Ben that we could have? Oh, and if you've got one of Jimmy the gardener too that would be great,' Dan asked.

'Jimmy? Isn't he in yet? He's usually in early, around six thirty as a rule. He's such a nice man. You don't think that he's got anything to do with this dreadful business?' Alice asked with a worried expression.

'It's just routine,' Dan said reassuringly.

'Not much luck there then,' Dan said once Alice had left the kitchen to look for photographs.

She came back a few minutes later with a photo in a frame.

'I thought that we had one in the conservatory somewhere,' she said with a smile as she passed the frame to Dan. 'That's Eleanor with Cathy and you can see Ben on the right and that's Jimmy in the back-ground.'

Dan passed the photo to Andy who eventually passed it to Mac. Cathy and a woman in her fifties were on the left and Ben was behind her on the right. The woman had greying hair, a well-cut black business suit and she wore black rimmed glasses. It was obviously a hot day as Ben was stripped to the waist and his muscular torso was glistening with sweat. In the background a man leant on a fork. He had a baseball cap on and he was smiling. Mac brought the photo closer for a better look and then groaned.

'What is it?' Dan asked. 'What have you noticed?'

'The gardener, James Stourton. Except that wasn't his name when I knew him.'

'You know the gardener?' Dan asked excitedly.

'I knew him professionally you might say. We've had one or two run-ins over the years but I knew him then as James Carmichael. He was quite famous for a while. He was suspected of cracking quite a few high-profile safes...'

'That's right he was supposed to have done that private bank in London,' Andy said. 'He didn't steal anything he just poured acid into a load of safety deposit boxes and scarpered. What was it they used to call him in the papers?'

'The Taxman, Robber Red, the socialist safecracker, amongst other things,' Mac repliid. 'His trade mark was leaving a note saying 'You have been taxed'. One of the newspapers noticed that large cash donations were made to several homeless charities after each burglary but of course nothing could be proved.'

'So, how did you become involved with him? He wasn't in the frame for a murder, was he?' Dan asked.

'No, in fact it was exactly the opposite. It was largely down to him that we cracked a case of attempted murder,' Mac replied.

'Tell me about it,' Dan asked.

'Okay then,' Mac said. 'One Friday night around ten o'clock, some seven years ago or so, Jimmy was in the process of opening a safe in Hatton Garden when he heard something from the room next door. He'd planned the robbery very carefully and he'd been following the owner of the premises for over a month. He knew the owner, a Mr. Carlyle, should have been safely tucked up in a gentleman's club in Pall Mall where he stayed without fail every Friday evening. So, he was surprised when he peeked around the office door and saw the said Mr. Carlyle lying on the floor. Jimmy could see that he was in a bad way. His skin was cold and clammy and his breath was very weak. He called 999 and, to give him his due, he waited until the ambulance showed up. Once they were on the scene he slipped out of the back window, the same way that he'd gotten in.'

'How did you find all this out?' Dan asked.

'He told me about it himself. About half an hour after slipping out the window he rang and asked to meet me in a pub. He was honest and said that he'd been after a batch of cut diamonds which he'd discovered had been delivered from Amsterdam to Mr. Carlyle the day before and that he was all set for a nice evening of safe cracking. Apparently, the safe was one that he hadn't come across before and so he was quite looking forward to the challenge.

He said that the reason he'd called me was because there was something really wrong about the whole thing. For a start he'd had to pick the lock of the front door of the offices so the ambulance men could get in. He couldn't find any keys for the door, not in the office

61

or in Mr. Carlyle's clothing. He also told me that Mr. Carlyle was a diabetic and he'd had a severe attack of hypoglycaemia, that's extremely low blood sugar, but he thought it was strange. The man was clutching a roll of high glucose tablets and Jimmy could see traces of them around the man's mouth. Jimmy put two more in and he knew that the man's condition should have improved a little but it didn't.'

'So, how would he know about all that?' Andy asked.

'Apparently his older brother is a diabetic,' Mac replied. 'He grew up with it and he recognised the symptoms straight away. He knew that Carlyle was worth millions which, after all, was why he was robbing him. However, he thought that there was something fishy going on and that I should know about it.

After I spoke to him, I went straight to the hospital and found that Mr. Carlyle was thankfully out of danger. The doctor told me that he'd been very lucky. If Jimmy hadn't come across him then he'd have been dead before morning. I asked if anyone had contacted his family and, thankfully, no-one had. As I was saying Jimmy had been watching Carlyle for a while and he had a theory.

I decided to trust him and so my sergeant and I found ourselves early the next morning camped out in Mr. Carlyle's office. I made sure the front door was locked and we waited in the side room which contained the safe. I left the door slightly open so I could peek through into the main office. About ten o'clock a key rattled in the lock of the front door and a woman walked in. She had a look of surprise on her face as she glanced around the office. She then opened the door of the office where we were waiting.

'He's not here,' I said.

The woman nearly jumped out of her skin. I flashed my warrant card and her face turned white. We took her down to the station and it wasn't long before she confessed. She, of course, was Mrs. Carlyle. She was a lot younger than her husband and had apparently gotten fed up waiting for him to die and decided to take matters into her own hands. It was simple really, she'd arranged for Mr. Carlyle's secretary to have the day off and so her husband was alone in the office. He always ate a packed lunch so that he could be sure he was taking enough carbohydrate in his food to keep his blood sugars up. Of course, she'd packed it for him. She made sure that it would be low in carbohydrates and she'd also made sure that he'd taken a little extra insulin as well. She knew then that he'd be very likely to have an attack of hypoglycaemia at some point that day. That's normally not such a big deal for diabetics so long as they can get some sugar into their system fairly quickly.'

'Let me guess,' said Dan. 'I'd bet that the so-called glucose tablets had no glucose in them.'

'Spot on,' Mac said. 'She'd found some sugar-free sweets that looked similar and swapped them for the real thing. When Mr. Carlyle felt the attack coming, he'd automatically taken a couple of the sweets and he should have been alright a few minutes later. I asked the doctor why Mr. Carlyle hadn't phoned for help. He said that unfortunately one of the side effects of the attack is mental confusion. The brain is starved of glucose and so you can't always think straight. That's then followed by a coma and, if left long enough, death. We found out later that she'd checked the office on Friday evening and saw him lying unconscious on the floor. He was in a coma but still alive. So, she took his keys and just left him there, locking the door behind her to be on the safe side.

She'd planned it beautifully. She'd arrive on Saturday morning, unlock the door and find him dead. After swapping the fake glucose tablets for the real ones she could then call for help knowing that the only possible verdict would be death from natural causes. She'd play the weeping widow for a while before disappearing

63

into the sunset with all her husband's money. It was just pure luck that saved her husband's life.'

'So, what happened after that?' Dan asked.

'Well, a couple of nights afterwards someone broke into Mr. Carlyle's safe and then made off with around a hundred thousand pounds worth of diamonds. He left a note saying 'You have been taxed'. I must admit that Mr. Carlyle wasn't very upset about it when I told him about the robbery. All he said was, 'He's earned it'.'

'Bloody hell, you know some good stories,' Dan said admiringly.

'So, will you when you've been around as long as I have. However, the point of the story is that, although Jimmy was a burglar, I don't think he's a killer. He has this weird sense of morality that wouldn't let him do anything like that. Anyway, he was never into art, only money or things that he could easily turn into money.'

'People change,' Dan said. 'Ben might have surprised him, who knows? Anyway, someone like him working as a gardener, does that seem right to you?'

'It does actually. I saw him not too long ago when he helped me out with a case and he said that he'd learnt all about gardening in prison and he'd come to love it. He told me that he'd been looking for work as a gardener but he hadn't had any luck. Obviously, his luck changed.'

'Isn't him changing his name a bit suspicious too?' Dan persisted.

'I have to admit that it could be,' Mac conceded. 'I didn't realise that he'd changed his name but, personally, I'd bet that he had a good reason for doing it.'

'By the way what was the case that he helped you with?' Dan asked.

'The Pierson case[1], you know the famous local painter. One of his daughters was robbing his estate blind. Anyway, Jimmy cracked the painter's safe for me and

---

[1] The Weeping Women – the third Mac Maguire mystery

that's how we got the evidence that we needed to convict her.'

'Oh yes, I remember that one. She got six years in the end, didn't she?' Dan said.

They were interrupted by Ben Yeardley, the head of the forensics team, who told them what they'd found so far. Ben Meeks had been killed no later than one in the morning by several very heavy blows to the left side of the skull with a blunt instrument. The weapon hadn't been found and the body hadn't been moved. That was basically it. It had been a very professional job.

'Does that mean that his attacker was likely to be right-handed?' Dan asked.

'Possibly, however the attacker might have been left-handed and hit the deceased from behind. We might know more after the autopsy's taken place,' Ben replied.

'Are we okay to have a look around?' Dan asked.

'Yes, we've moved the body but try not to disturb things too much just in case we need to come back. Here make sure you put these on too,' Ben said as he handed them a pair of latex gloves each.

He picked up his big black case and left them to it.

'Well, that rules Johnny Kinsella out as we know that he was at a party in London until two o'clock and with Cathy Conyers in Manchester, the assistant on a cruise and the cook in Cambridge, then that just leaves the gardener,' Dan said pointedly. 'So, for now at least, Mr. Carmichael is a suspect. In fact, he looks like he's our only suspect.'

Mac couldn't fault Dan's logic. He looked down at the second blood stained carpet he'd seen that day and sighed. While Dan and Andy were busy looking around the house Mac thought his time might be better spent finding out more about Jimmy Carmichael and what he was doing working as a gardener. He told Dan that he was going to have another word with the cook and left them to it.

He asked Alice where Jimmy worked and she took him some two hundred yards down the garden to a large shed that was hidden behind a tree. Mac had to take it slowly and found he was dazzled by the beauty and the colours of the plants around him, most of which he was fairly certain that he'd never seen before. Such colour surprised him. It was as though he'd been transported to the tropics. He thought how much his wife would have loved being shown around such a beautiful garden. The shed door was locked but the cook felt along a narrow ledge above the door and produced a key. Mac put on the gloves before he took it from her.

'Thanks Alice,' Mac said. 'I won't keep you and I'll be sure to lock up after myself.'

He watched her walk back towards the house before he turned and went inside. Hot air flowed around him as he walked inside and he broke into a sudden sweat. Two large windows on one side of the shed provided more than enough light and, in this case, heat. On one side a long workbench ran underneath the windows on which several small hand tools and a stack of empty seed trays were neatly arranged. On the other side the whole wall was covered with garden tools of every sort, each hanging on its own peg. Mac had to admit that the shed was probably tidier than most people's houses.

There were a series of drawers underneath the bench. Mac took his time going through each one. He found nothing out of the ordinary until he came to the last but one. While the others had various items of gardening paraphernalia, tools and packets of seeds, this one was stuffed with pieces of paper.

He looked through the papers most of which were rough designs for flower beds or other garden features. However, Mac's heart skipped a beat when he came to a plan that definitely wasn't anything to do with gardening.

It was a sort of electrical diagram most of which made no sense to Mac except for a section marked 'fingerprint

66

sensor'. Mac would bet that it was a schematic of the security system. He poked around the drawer with a pen and found a clear plastic bag with a hypodermic needle and an empty phial of something called Tiletamine. Mac bent down and read the label carefully. It said that it was a sedative and was only to be used on animals.

So that's what happened to Charmaine, Mac thought. He found himself feeling quite disappointed. For all that they had been on opposite sides of the fence, he'd found that he quite liked Jimmy Carmichael but what had he gone and done now?

Did the Taxman really have blood on his hands?

Chapter Eight

Mac immediately showed Dan and Andy what he'd found. They were quite delighted with his finds but he didn't take any pleasure in it at all.

'Do you still think that Jimmy's not involved?' Dan asked as they stood in the garden just outside the shed.

'Well, it looks damning I know but...'

'You still don't think it's him, do you?' Dan said as he gave Mac a look of disbelief.

'Come here,' Mac said as he stepped back into the heat of the shed. 'In all of the robberies that the Taxman carried out not one scrap of evidence was ever found; no tools, no fingerprints, no DNA, absolutely nothing. Now, just look at this place, the place where Jimmy worked. It's a garden shed yet it's absolutely spotless with everything exactly in its place. Do you really think that someone like that would really leave such damning evidence lying about in a drawer for us to find?'

'Well, you might have a point there,' Dan said, 'but, if he's as innocent as you claim, then why has he done a runner? Everyone makes a mistake sometimes Mac, even you. Perhaps Jimmy did too, except this mistake will get him a lifetime in jail.'

Mac couldn't say any more and he had to admit to himself that Dan was absolutely right. While, for some reason he was trying to convince himself that Jimmy couldn't have committed such a crime, he also had to admit that, if he was back in the force and in Dan's place, he'd be hunting Jimmy down with all of his might.

Mac said his goodbyes. It was a straight manhunt now and, as he didn't have the heart for it, he left them to it. Dan thanked him for his help and promised to keep him up to date with any developments. He turned it all over in his mind as he drove back to Letchworth.

It had only just gone three o'clock. Mac popped in to see Father Pat and told him about his visit to Albert Ginn's house. With a hint of desperation, he asked if the priest had remembered anything new, anything that might help his case. He hadn't. Mac left feeling a bit down and frustrated.

He pondered on what to do next. An old friend of his used to say, 'If in doubt, go to the pub' and Mac decided to once again take his advice. He called on Tim who was more than happy to knock off early and so, by four o'clock, Mac was comfortably cocooned in the Magnets with an ice-cold pint of lager in front of him waiting to be despatched.

Mac knew that in coming to the pub he wasn't totally downing tools. He needed to talk to someone about the two cases and see if he could get a different angle on things.

Mac had a sad moment as he realised that his late wife, Nora, had always been the first person he'd go to when he got stuck on a case. She always seemed to be able to see things that Mac hadn't noticed. Still he knew that he should count his blessings and be glad that he had such a good friend as Tim to talk things through with.

While he gratefully sipped at his lager, Mac took Tim through the circumstances around Father Pat's case.

Tim was thoughtful for a while.

'You know, I can't help thinking that your man Adil might not have been too far off the mark.'

'You mean in saying that Father Pat did it and is even denying it to himself? Yes, I must admit that it's crossed my mind more than once,' Mac said.

'I know Father Pat's a good man but it's the time factor that's making me think that. How could anyone have gotten into the room and killed Albert Ginn in the time it took Father Pat to reach the front door? If, as you say,

69

the place is like a fortress then I just can't see how it could have been done.'

Mac glumly conceded the point. He then told Tim all about the murder of Ben Meeks and the theft of the painting.

'Well, if you think it's an inside job then it has to be the actress, the cook, the chauffeur or the gardener.'

'Or the rock star,' Mac added.

'Yes, I was forgetting about Johnny. It's like something from an Agatha Christie novel, isn't it?' Tim grinned. 'If you're going to get them all together in a country house and then reveal the murderer, please make sure that I get an invite, will you?'

Mac smiled and then his face clouded over again.

'Unfortunately, the gardener looks the best bet.'

'Why unfortunately?'

'Because, if I'm absolutely honest, I quite like him,' Mac replied. 'He was a thief alright but he never stole for himself and the people he stole from could all well afford it. He had his own rules and, as far as I know, he always stuck to them. In all his robberies there was never any violence involved.'

'So, although he's robbed loads of people in the past, you don't like him for this one?' Tim asked.

'No, I don't but it's only based on what I know about Jimmy. I've absolutely no evidence otherwise.'

'So, if he's not guilty then why has he done a runner?'

'That's the question,' Mac replied. 'Dan's convinced it must be him. He's got a record and he had the opportunity. There's even some hard evidence against him. Yet...'

'Yet you still don't think it's him, do you?' Tim said.

'No, I don't. Any ideas?' Mac asked hopefully.

'Follow the money,' Tim suggested.

'Follow the money? What money?' Mac said with a puzzled expression.

'I only meant it metaphorically. Remember that film 'All the President's Men' about where they got the goods on President Nixon?'

Mac nodded not having a clear idea where Tim was going with this.

'Well, they were trying to find a way through a very complex case and they weren't sure which way to go,' Tim explained. 'So, the informer, Deep Throat, tells them to follow the money. Just forget everything else and concentrate on that one facet of the investigation.'

'I think I see what you're getting at. What's the single facet of this case that I should be concentrating on then?' Mac asked.

Tim shrugged his shoulders.

'How should I know? You're the detective.'

While part of Mac didn't think this very helpful, another part stored the thought away for later.

Mac noticed that their glasses were empty and got up to go to the bar. When he returned, he decided to change the subject. He gave Tim the autograph and told him about meeting Johnny Kinsella and how they had both been invited to a boy's night in with the famous rock star. Tim was absolutely thrilled.

'God, I can't believe it. I'm actually going to meet Johnny Kinsella!' Tim enthused. 'I tried to get a ticket for his charity gig last night but they'd sold out in minutes. This will be even better though.'

'That's if it's still on with this murder and everything. I'll try and ring him in a few days but don't get your hopes up too high,' Mac warned. 'Anyway, enough of murders and rock stars let's talk about something really serious. What the hell is going on at Aston Villa? How could they lose a home game against that bunch of amateurs when they'd just beaten the league leaders away the week before?'

As always talking about football provided a topic of conversation that not only lasted them all night but could have kept them going all week. The evening passed more than comfortably by as they satisfactorily solved all of their favourite club's defensive frailties.

Mac woke up the following morning just after eight o'clock, feeling slightly muzzy after his night with Tim. He gingerly sat up and checked his pain levels before standing up. He experienced a bit of a sharp twinge but, all in all, it wasn't too bad. So, he showered and shaved and then had his breakfast standing up by the kitchen window. He watched the birds outside in the garden as they queued up at the bird feeders. His wife Nora had loved watching the different types of birds as they hung from the feeder or pecked around for the seeds that she always threw on the lawn. Mac's reverie was broken by the phone ringing.

It was Dan and he sounded happy.

'Mac, we've got Jimmy Carmichael!'

'How?'

'You won't believe it but he walked into the incident room about half an hour ago and gave himself up.'

'I must admit that was the last thing I was expecting,' Mac said.

'I'd be grateful if you could come over Mac,' Dan asked. 'I've tried to question him but he won't say a word, he just keeps asking to see you.'

'I'll be right there.'

Mac made it to the incident room within half an hour, good going for his ageing Almera. The incident room proved to be a part of the local pub 'The Bricket Arms'. However, there was to be a little less temptation for the investigators as it was in a separate building on the other side of the car park from the pub, one that was normally used for weddings and other events. Three uniformed officers were trying to keep the tide of the press and other onlookers at bay. A barrage of flashes went off as Mac drove into the car park.

It hasn't taken them long, Mac thought. He thought of Dan and wished him luck. He'd need it with this case being so much in the media spotlight.

Dan looked pleased to see him.

'Not bad this,' Mac said as he looked around.

Most of the team seemed to be there and there was plenty of room for everyone. There were even a couple of smaller rooms leading off the main one that were being used as interview rooms.

'Yes, Adil did a good job,' Dan said. 'I must admit that I was a bit sceptical at first when he said it was a pub. Not only that but they've got some rooms over the pub as well. So, I've booked a couple just in case anyone needs to stay late.'

'Did anything else happen yesterday after I left?' Mac asked.

'Well, we were able to interview Cathy Conyers at last. She got back around five o'clock yesterday. She was very upset about her painting being stolen and even more so when she learnt that Ben Meeks was dead. I told her that she couldn't go back to the house for a while yet as it's still a crime scene, so she's taken a room at the Grange Hall Hotel.'

This didn't surprise Mac. The Grange Hall was probably the most expensive hotel in the county.

'Did you get anything from her?'

Dan shook his head.

'No, nothing really, apart from the fact that she said that she wasn't aware of Jimmy Carmichael's real name or his criminal past. Anyway, she promised that she'd hang around for a couple of days in case we needed her. Johnny Kinsella contacted us as well. He said that he'd come in later today so we'll see what his involvement is, if any.'

Dan stopped outside one of the small rooms. It had a handwritten notice pinned to the door 'Interview Room 1'.

'Mac, as you know Jimmy Carmichael, I'd be grateful if you could take the lead and try and get what you can from him. I think that we might have enough evidence to prosecute but a bit more definitely wouldn't hurt.'

Mac nodded but said nothing. He wasn't sure if he wanted to be the person who put Jimmy Carmichael behind bars but, if he found that he really had killed Ben Meeks, he knew that he'd have no compunctions about it either.

Jimmy sat straight backed and didn't move when the door opened. Mac sat down opposite him.

Dan was about to sit down too when Jimmy said, 'Not you, only Mr. Maguire.'

Dan glanced at Mac, nodded and left the room. Mac looked Jimmy over. He hadn't changed that much from the young man that Mac had first met some years before. He still had the same slim, wiry frame and stern features. The only difference that Mac could detect was that, even though he couldn't have been older than thirty, his short black hair was going slightly grey in places. He didn't move about or fidget as many people would have done in his situation. His hands rested in his lap and his body was completely still. His face, as always, gave absolutely nothing away.

'Mr. Maguire, as you're a private detective nowadays I want to hire you. I want you to find out who killed Ben Meeks.'

Mac was surprised at Jimmy's request and he had to give it some thought. He knew that Dan and the team would never knowingly try to railroad anyone into a conviction but he had to admit that the evidence was stacking up against Jimmy. It was lucky for him that Mac didn't believe any of it.

'Before I give you an answer to that I want you to look me in the eye and say that you didn't kill Ben Meeks.'

Jimmy gazed unflinchingly at Mac.

'I didn't kill Ben Meeks or have anything to do with the theft of Cathy's painting.'

Mac smiled with relief.

'Okay, I believe you.'

'So, you'll work for me?' Jimmy asked.

Mac sat thinking for a while.

'No, that's not something I can do. The people out there are the team I work with. I can't just say that I'm swapping sides and go and work for their main suspect. I hope you can see that. However, I promise that I'll do my best to find out the truth about who really killed Ben Meeks. Do you believe me?'

Jimmy gave Mac a searching look before nodding.

'I do.'

'Okay then, what can you tell me?' Mac asked.

'I don't know much really,' Jimmy said. 'I certainly don't know anything about security schematics or dog sedatives. It was total news to me when Mr. Carter told me about finding those in the shed.'

'It was me who found them but my first thought was that it was a plant,' Mac said. 'I couldn't believe that someone as meticulous as you could ever be that sloppy.'

'Thanks. If I'd have carried out the theft no-one would have been hurt, apart from Miss Conyers' insurance company perhaps, and they can afford it.'

'Have you ever considered stealing the painting?'

Jimmy shook his head.

'It's never even crossed my mind, not once. I need you to understand that, even when I was stealing, I never needed the money for myself. Cathy pays me enough and she's a good boss. She's never once interfered with what I do in the garden, she just lets me get on with things.'

'So, how did you end up being her gardener?' Mac asked.

'Ben Meeks got me the job. He told me that he was getting a promotion and that he'd put a good word in for me. I'd told him that I'd been to prison, I've never lied to anyone about that, but he said that he was sure that Miss Conyers wouldn't mind. He must have been right because I got the job.'

'So, as far as you're concerned Ben told Cathy Conyers about your record?' Mac asked.

'That's what he told me.'

Mac was thoughtful for a moment.

'How did you get to know Ben?'

'I met him at my local pub, The Apple Tree,' Jimmy replied. 'Although he lived at Cathy's house, he still visited his old local in Welwyn from time to time. We both liked watching sport on the TV they had there and we'd chat about the games or the races as we watched them. He became quite friendly after we had a session one night. I'd been made redundant and so I'd decided to drown my sorrows. I told him all about it and how hard it would be for me to find another job with my record. He asked me what I really wanted to do. I told him that I'd been working nights in a warehouse and that I'd basically hated every minute of it. I said that what I'd really like to be was a gardener. I'd spent most of my time in prison looking after the gardens and I'd really gotten into it. Watching things grow had some-how helped with the constant anger I'd felt inside.'

'Tell me, why were you so angry?'

Mac was really interested in what had driven Jimmy to commit such crimes in the first place.

'When I was young, we were dirt poor. My dad had done a runner and my mum did her best but there were many times when there just wasn't enough to go around. She always made sure that my brother and I had something to eat but she'd often go without. We were even homeless on a few occasions and, if it hadn't been for the charities, I don't know what we'd have done.

When I was fourteen, she died and we went to live with my dad. He was a right piece of work; a thief, a con

76

man, he'd do anything to make money, apart from work that is. It was dad that started me on the safe cracking although he wasn't much good at it himself. I became interested and even more so when I came across this old guy who had a reputation as a cracker when he'd been younger. He was good to me and taught me a lot about safes and how to finesse them open. So, eventually I went into business for myself but I also worked part-time for one of the homeless charities that had helped us when I'd been younger. I reckoned I owed them.

The misery you see there is appalling, especially the kids. Just a few quid would have solved most of their problems, yet you see such wealth all around you. So, as I didn't need the money and neither did the rich people I robbed, I decided that some forced giving to charity might help balance the scales a bit. Of course, it was just a piss in the ocean but it helped me stay sane for a while.

Then I got caught and, looking back, it was probably one of the best things that ever happened to me. I spent most of my sentence in an open prison where I was assigned to the gardens. I surprised myself by getting to really like the work. I started reading all the books I could lay my hands on and I even started listening to Gardeners' Question Time on the radio if you can believe that. I became a bit of an expert and the prison garden even won some local awards while I was in charge of it. The only problem was that I couldn't get any work as a gardener when I got out. Even after I changed my name, the only job I could get was working nights in a warehouse and even that didn't last long.'

'Why exactly did you change your name?' Mac asked.

'I wanted a new start, a new life I suppose and having the name of Carmichael hasn't ever done me any favours. When I got married, I changed my surname to my wife's by deed poll. Her mum and dad have been very good to me too, so I really didn't mind being called

Stourton. Anyway, as I said it didn't seem to be helping much but then, within a couple of weeks of being made redundant, I found myself working in Cathy Conyers' garden. I just couldn't believe my luck. She was really good to me. She let me have my head and luckily she liked what I did.'

'It's a very beautiful garden,' Mac said.

'Thanks. I was happy, possibly for the first time in my life. I'd met my wife Danielle just before I got caught and went into prison. I swore to myself that it was going to be my final job, and I suppose it was, just not in the way I'd figured. Well, she visited me in jail every chance she got and she stuck with me. Eighteen months she waited and I swore to myself I'd never put her through that again. And then Jenny, my little daughter came along, and that made us complete. I'd never put all that in jeopardy for a painting or for all the money in the world.'

'I believe you, Jimmy. Tell me more about Ben.'

'He seemed okay, a bit out for himself maybe, but he was mad on Cathy,' Jimmy said. 'He'd have done anything for her.'

'And how did Miss Conyers treat him?'

'Like a chauffeur,' Jimmy replied. 'Although he was young and good looking, I don't think she ever gave him a second look.'

'And how did Ben take that?' Mac asked.

'Not well. I've seen him look quite sourly at Cathy but then he'd make a laugh of it. I think he was a bit resentful of her at times though.'

'Resentful enough to steal her painting perhaps?'

Jimmy shrugged.

'Who knows what goes on in people's heads? I doubt we ever really saw the true Ben but, as I said, I think that he really did care for Cathy in his own way. Anyway, I know that it wasn't me who got rid of the dog or planted that stuff in the shed so that pretty much just leaves Ben, doesn't it?'

Mac nodded. He was beginning to feel the same.

'Okay, I think my first job is to find out as much as I can about the real Mr. Meeks,' Mac said. 'Have you any ideas about where I should start?'

'Try the pub. Ben had been going there for quite a while before I started using it. He used to talk to the landlord a lot. His name's Bill Simmonds. Perhaps he might know something.'

Mac nodded. He'd always found pub landlords to have a surprising breadth of knowledge about their patrons. After all they were the ones who had to stay sober most of the time.

'Just one more question,' Mac said. 'Was it you who tipped off the police about Ben's murder?'

Jimmy nodded.

'I went to work as usual yesterday but when I got there the gate was open and so was the front door. I went in and looked around and that's when I found Ben lying dead on the floor and the painting gone. With my record I knew that I'd automatically be in the frame for it. I called the police and then went back home. I told Danielle what had happened and we quickly agreed a plan. We packed some things and I drove her over to her parents' house in Stevenage. We both knew that there was a possibility that the police wouldn't look past me, so we decided to have one last night together before I handed myself in.'

'You were wise to do that. Don't worry Jimmy, I'll do my best for you,' Mac promised.

'Thanks, Mr. Maguire. I'm sure that your best will be more than good enough.'

Mac wished he was as confident in his abilities as Jimmy was. He took his leave and went to see Dan.

'What did he say? Was there anything we can use?' Dan asked in anticipation.

'No, nothing really. He told me that he didn't kill Ben Meeks and, if I'm honest, I believe him,' Mac said. 'After all it was him who called it in. I haven't heard of many murderers who've done that.'

'You really don't think it's him, do you Mac?' Dan asked.

'No, I don't, I just wish that I had a shred of evidence to back me up but we are where we are.'

'So, what do you want to do?'

'I'd like to look a bit more closely at Ben Meeks if that's okay with you,' Mac replied. 'When we met, I got the distinct feeling that something about him didn't quite ring true.'

Dan gave it some thought.

'That sounds fair enough. The rest of the team will be concentrating on Jimmy though as my boss would want to know why otherwise. However, it definitely wouldn't hurt to have a plan B just in case you're right. If you want to help out, I could spare Kate for a few days. What do you think?'

'Kate? Kate Grimsson?' Mac said with a surprised expression. 'Is she working for you now?'

'She's just starting today as luck would have it.'

'How on earth did that come about?' Mac asked in some wonder.

'Well, I think that we were all impressed with her work on the Whyte case and I got the impression that she wasn't too happy where she was,' Dan explained. 'So, when Martina got her promotion and left us for the Rape Team, I asked her if she was interested.'

'I take it that she was interested then?' Mac asked.

'She just about bit my hand off. I was going to partner her with Tommy as they'd worked so well together but, as he'll be lying on a beach somewhere for the next few weeks, then she's free.'

'That would be great. So where is she now?' Mac asked as he looked around the room.

'She's doing a handover of the case that she's been working on in Hatfield but she should be on her way over here shortly.'

While he waited Mac said hello to the rest of the team and caught up on the latest news. Jo reminded him once again of the date of the wedding. Mac promised that he'd be there but he could sense that Jo was getting worried about the case dragging on too long and spoiling her big day.

Kate turned up half an hour later looking uncertain and flustered. She disappeared into an interview room with Dan for ten minutes and came out looking somewhat calmer. Her eyes searched the room and, when they found Mac, her face lit up and she flashed him a smile.

Strange looking as Kate was, with her flame red hair and snow-white skin, Mac thought she looked quite lovely at that moment. He thought of the wry smile that his wife Nora used to give him when she caught him looking at another, usually younger, woman.

'It's only theoretical,' he used to say, 'like looking at a nice work of art.'

And it really had been. There had only ever been one woman in the world that Mac had felt really passionate about. However, he couldn't help noticing that these days it had become even more theoretical than ever and he was more than happy to keep it that way.

Kate had worked with Mac on a cold case while he'd been confined to bed for several weeks. She'd worked very hard and very successfully too. Mac had high hopes for her.

She came over and shook his hand.

'It's nice to see you again, Mac, and out of bed too,' she said with a big smile.

'It's nice to see you too, Kate. I've only just heard about you joining the team. Congratulations.'

'Thanks, it was an easy decision to make. So, we're working together again then,' she said with a smile.

'Dan tells me that we're looking at the man who was murdered.'

'Yes, Jimmy Carmichael, our main suspect, has given me some information that we need to follow up on. I've got a feeling that there's a lot more to Ben Meeks than we've discovered so far.'

Chapter Nine

Mac had only just made it into the pub's car park when his phone rang. Kate looked over at Mac as he listened.

'That was Cathy Conyers and she wants to see us right away,' Mac said as he put his phone away.

'Well, let's not keep the Queen of Soaps waiting then,' Kate replied with a grin.

As they drove towards the hotel Mac asked, 'Why did you call her that?'

'What, the Queen of Soaps? She was voted that in a magazine recently. Not that I keep up with that sort of thing generally.'

Mac gave her a look but said nothing.

'Well okay, I do keep up with that sort of thing actually. Being alone in the evening it's something to do,' she admitted.

'So, you follow the soap that Cathy Conyers stars in?'

'Yes, I have to admit that I do,' she said with a frown.

'It's not a crime you know and, in fact, I'm glad that you do. You never know but it might help with the case in some way.'

Cathy Conyers' room at the hotel was as grand as her living room but Mac could see that the grand dame had disappeared leaving a dazed and vulnerable looking middle-aged woman in her place.

She looked relieved to see him but seemed somewhat surprised at seeing Kate follow him in. Mac told Cathy that he was working with the police now and introduced Kate.

'Mr. Maguire, it's really good of you to come so quickly. I just can't believe…I just can't make sense out of any of this,' she said as she paced anxiously up and down the room. 'I so wish Eleanor were here, she'd know what to do.'

'Have you spoken to her yet?' Mac asked.

'No, I've had my phone switched off but we've been able to exchange a few emails. She wanted to come back but I told her not to. I couldn't see the point especially as it would take her a couple of days before she could even get off the ship as it's between islands. Anyway, what could she do? What can anyone do?'

She sat down for a moment and then quickly stood back up and started pacing again.

'Mr. Maguire, I know that you used to investigate murder cases when you were in the police and I feel responsible somehow. I just want to know what happened to Ben.'

'Didn't the police tell you anything when they spoke to you yesterday?' Mac asked.

'Not really, just that Ben was dead, the painting had gone and that they were questioning someone. They said that they'd let me know more 'in due course' whatever that meant.'

Mac gave himself a while to think it through and then decided that he might as well tell her what he knew.

'The security system was disabled and your painting was stolen. We think that Ben was killed during the robbery. He was hit on the left side of his head several times with a blunt instrument. They found some evidence in the shed where Jimmy worked; a plan of the security system, a syringe and a phial of a drug called Tiletamine. Apparently, it's used for sedating animals.'

'Is that what happened to Charmaine? Was she was sedated before she disappeared?' she asked.

'Quite possibly. This was an expert job and experts always try and reduce the risks. Dogs, especially big dogs like Charmaine, are always a risk. You can never be sure of what they might do next.'

'Do the police really think that Jimmy did it?'

Mac nodded.

'Yes, and they think that they have enough evidence to make a good case too.'

'I find it so hard to believe,' Cathy said as she shook her head. 'Jimmy was so gentle with those plants. I watched him sometimes as he worked, he so loved that garden. Yet the police say that he was a criminal, a thief.'

'Didn't Ben say anything about Jimmy's record when he suggested Jimmy as his replacement?' Mac asked.

'No. The police asked me that too. Why would Ben have kept that from me?'

'Would you have employed Jimmy if he had?'

Cathy thought for a moment.

'If I'm being absolutely honest, probably not.'

'Perhaps he was just trying to help a friend or...'

Mac stopped in mid-sentence. He'd had a thought.

'Or what?' she asked.

'Oh, nothing really. How well did you know Ben?' Mac asked.

'Not that well I suppose,' Cathy said. 'He was recommended as a gardener by a friend of mine and he was a good worker. He always kept the garden nice and tidy but that was about it. When Jimmy came it was as though the garden came to life somehow. I think that he's a bit of a genius when it comes to plants and garden design. Anyway, Ben had been with me nearly eighteen months when Johnny and I split up. I decided that I needed a chauffeur as I don't drive myself and Ben was more than happy to volunteer.'

'What about his background?'

'He came from the same area of Manchester as I do. To be honest that was probably the main reason why I warmed to him. He moved down here around six years ago with his mother. She died about four years ago.'

'He had no other family?' Mac asked.

'Not as far as I know, apart from an aunt in Salford that is,' she replied. 'But I don't remember him ever going to visit her.'

Mac thought back to his conversation with Ben.

'Why did Johnny think that you and Ben were having an affair?'

Cathy's face started to crumple but she just about managed to keep the tears at bay.

'Because I told him we were.'

'But you weren't, so why would you tell him that?' Mac asked.

She pulled a newspaper from a pile that lay on the bed. She passed it to Mac.

'Because of her.'

Mac looked at the same photo that he'd seen on Andy's mobile phone. The picture here was much larger and Mac had to admit the girl looked even more stunning. The headline was 'Mystery Girl - Is this Johnny's new love?'

'Who is she?' Mac asked.

'I've no idea. About a year ago Johnny starting acting strangely. There were mysterious letters and phone calls then he'd disappear for a while and come back with some lame excuse. Then, one day, I caught him just sitting there with this stupid grin on his face and I knew.'

'You thought that he was having an affair, didn't you?' Mac said.

'No, I knew that he was having an affair,' she almost shouted. 'I got a detective from London to follow Johnny and he saw him with this particular young lady three times in all. They were quite affectionate too or so he said. The last time he took her to that stately pile he has near St. Albans and they were there for over two days and two nights, of course. When Johnny came home, he found his bags were packed and I told him to leave. I told him that Ben and I loved each other and that I wanted a divorce. A pathetic lie I know but I didn't want to be the one who was dumped.'

'How did he take it?'

'I must admit that he surprised me. I thought that he'd be glad for an excuse to go but he seemed really upset and, I don't know, shocked I suppose. I just thought that he wanted to have his cake and eat it. To have me and his bit on the side as well. Anyway, I filed for a divorce immediately. He didn't contest it,' she said with a look of disappointment.

'And keeping the dog was one way of getting back at him,' Mac stated.

'Yes, I was being a bit petty I suppose but there you are. Anyway, enough of my troubles,' she said as she wiped a tear away. 'Have the police found Jimmy yet?'

'No, Jimmy found them. He handed himself in this morning.'

'Do you really think that Jimmy killed Ben?'

'No, I don't,' Mac replied. 'However, there's a lot of evidence against him at the moment.'

'Tell me about Jimmy, about his past,' she asked.

Mac told her everything that he knew about Jimmy Carmichael, including his conversation with him just before coming to see her.

She was thoughtful for a moment.

'Okay, from what you've said I don't think it's likely to be Jimmy either.'

Mac decided to ask a question that had been on his mind since he'd first seen the painting.

'Tell me, how did you happen to have such a valuable painting anyway? I know TV pays well but...'

'That's a story in itself,' she replied.

'Tell me the story,' Mac asked gently.

He was curious and it was always possible that the painting's history might shed some light on recent events.

With a sad smile Cathy started telling Mac her story.

'I was young and just getting into the business when I first met the owner of the painting. He was a lot older than me. I was doing a bit part in a film and he was the star. He'd done everything; theatre, British films and then he'd conquered Hollywood too. He was a real

87

charmer and I fell for him in a big way. He'd been buying works of art over the years and he had quite a collection. I remember the first time he showed me the Munch and how pleased he was when he saw how much I liked it. So, we had an affair and I fell deeply in love with him. It lasted nearly a year until one day he said it was over and he didn't want to see me again.'

She looked over at Mac with eyes brimming with tears.

'God, it still hurts now, even after all these years. So, you can believe how shocked and distraught I felt at the time. The pain was worse than I could have ever imagined,' she continued. 'Then, some seven or eight weeks later, he called me and asked me to visit him. In that short time, he'd changed remarkably. He'd lost weight and he looked like a shadow of the man I'd known. It was cancer, he told me, and he'd broken it off with me only because he thought it would be kinder than seeing him slowly die. It broke my heart seeing him like that but at least I knew that he cared for me and that helped. I stayed with him until he died some two weeks later. He had children, who got most of the estate, but he left me that painting. Him leaving it to me was his way of saying that he loved me. It was the first time I'd really loved anyone and I thought it might be the only time until I met Johnny. Poor Ben knew how important the painting was to me and he died trying to save it when all the time...' she left the sentence dangling.

A light bulb went on in Mac's head. He finished the sentence for her.

'When all the time it was just a copy?'

She flinched when he said this.

'Yes, you're right. The painting that was stolen was only a copy. I could never chance losing the real one. It means much more than money to me.'

'So, where's the real one?'

'It's in a bank vault in London,' Cathy replied.

'So why did you tell everyone that it was real?' Mac asked.

'To make me look more interesting I suppose, a lover of great art, someone…someone who wasn't me. And now Ben's dead and all because of my little lie. I daresay he wouldn't have risked his life trying to stop the thieves if he'd known that it was just a fake. So, you see, his death is all my fault really,' she said with a bleak look on her face.

'Have you told anyone else about this yet?' Mac asked.

Cathy shook her head. Mac thought furiously.

'How good a fake is it?' he asked.

'It's really good or so I've been told. It cost me well over ten thousand pounds and the artist swore that it would pass for real. I had some Munch experts look at it not long ago and they couldn't tell that it was a copy.'

'So, whoever stole it probably still thinks that they have the original. That could be really useful information. Can you keep this to yourself for now?' Mac asked. 'It's really important.'

'I'd be glad to,' Cathy replied. 'It's not something I'm particularly proud of anyway. What are you going to do now?'

'Try and find some evidence that proves that Jimmy didn't do it,' Mac replied. 'We're going to start by trying to find out a bit more about Ben.'

Cathy wished them luck and Mac and Kate took their leave. Just as they were going out of the door, Mac glanced back. Cathy Conyers stood facing the window, one hand on the window pane. In that moment she somehow looked very fragile.

By the time he made his way down to the street, he'd decided that he was beginning to like Cathy Conyers. He was just about to get into the car when his mobile rang again.

It was Adil.

'Mac, someone wants to speak to you.'

He heard the phone being passed over and then Johnny Kinsella's Brummie accent.

'Mac mate, how's Cathy? Have you seen her?'

'I've just come from her,' Mac replied. 'She's quite upset as you might guess. It's quite sad really. I don't think that she's got anyone to call on.'

'She's always got me,' Johnny said. 'Look, can you do me a big favour and take me to her? We can talk while you drive me there. I came in by taxi, I couldn't chance driving as I'm still quite a bit overhung from last night.'

'Sure.'

Mac told Kate that they were temporarily going to be a chauffeur service to the rich and famous.

'My God, first Cathy Conyers and now Johnny Kinsella as well. The Queen of Soaps and the King of Heavy Metal all in one day. It's a pity that I forgot to bring my autograph book with me,' she said feigning disappointment.

The mob outside the incident room had grown. There were now six uniformed policemen on duty and they had a job clearing the way for Kate to drive in. Johnny was waiting patiently in the incident room when they got there. He seemed glad to see Mac.

'How's Cathy?' he asked anxiously.

'She's not doing that well I think,' Mac replied. 'How did you get past that scrum out there?'

The crowd of pressmen and bystanders had grown and there were even a couple of TV vans out there now.

'The taxi driver put me in the boot. It's not the first time I've had to do that,' Johnny replied.

'Unfortunately for you it's not going to be the last time either,' Mac said. 'However, I need to have a word with someone before we go.'

He caught Dan's eye and went into one of the interview rooms. Dan followed him in.

'I've just been to see Cathy Conyers and she let something slip. The thief planned everything pretty much to

90

perfection, however, there's something quite important that he's overlooked. He's only stolen a copy.'

'A copy?' Dan exclaimed in surprise.

'Yes, it's a really good one though. The chances are that the thief doesn't know it yet.'

'Now that's a welcome bit of news and perhaps one that we could use to our benefit somehow,' Dan said.

'Yes, knowing something the criminal doesn't is always useful,' Mac said. 'I've asked Cathy Conyers to keep it to herself until she's told otherwise.'

'Good. Thanks for letting me know, Mac,' Dan said.

Mac went back into the incident room and saw that Johnny was still waiting patiently. Mac asked Kate to back the car up to a side door so that it was out of sight from the roadside where the gang of pressmen were gathered. Johnny expertly got himself in the boot.

Again, the camera flashes went off as they drove away but it was only perfunctory. A half a mile or so away Kate pulled off the road and checked to see if anyone was following. No-one was. She drove on until they came to a layby where she pulled in and let Johnny out.

He got in the back seat and Mac joined him there. He introduced him to Kate as they set off.

'Cheers Kate, has anyone ever told you that you're really unusual looking?' he asked quite bluntly.

Mac could see her eyes in the rear-view mirror. She obviously wasn't sure whether she should be offended or not.

'Yes, but not usually to my face,' she replied.

Her slightly sarcastic tone was lost on Johnny.

'We're doing a video for the new single soon,' Johnny said. 'Do you fancy being in it? I think you'd be great.'

'Yes, sure, I'd love to. That would be great,' Kate replied flashing Mac a look in the rear-view mirror which clearly asked whether Johnny was on something or just mad.

'Great!' Johnny replied.

As it wasn't such a long drive Mac thought they should get down to business.

'Tell me, why did you call me particularly? You must have lots of other people that you could have called instead.'

'I thought that there might be an outside chance you'd seen Cathy as you were working for her. I've been trying to call her for ages but her phone is switched off. She must be desperate, the man she loved being killed like that.'

'You still think she loved Ben?' Mac asked.

'Yes, she told me so herself,' Johnny said as he gave Mac a sad look.

'She and Ben were never lovers. She lied to you Johnny.'

Johnny looked at Mac in total mystification.

'Why would she say it then? I'm totally bloody confused now.'

'You were found out Johnny, she had you followed,' Mac said. 'I'm not the first detective she's hired. He saw you and that young girl together. Cathy knew that she'd stayed at your place in St. Albans with you for over two days or should I say two nights. She thought that she'd been traded in for a new model and all she was doing was getting her retaliation in first.'

'Bloody hell, I'd never have guessed that in a million years,' Johnny said with a bemused expression. 'I was so sure that she was in love with Ben but, then again, she is a good actress. I still love her Mac, never stopped, even when I thought...'

'So, why go out with this young girl then? Do you love her too?' Mac asked.

'I do love her, Mac. I love every bone in her body. I'd do absolutely anything for her.'

'You can't love two women Johnny. It never works out.'

Johnny shook his head.

'It's not like that, Mac. Let me tell you what happened.'

Chapter Ten

Mac was stunned by Johnny's story. He met Kate's eyes in the rear-view mirror and she raised her eyebrows at him. She was obviously surprised too.

'I promised her that I wouldn't tell anyone but I can see now that I should have told Cathy anyway. Husbands and wives shouldn't have secrets,' Johnny said.

'No, they shouldn't,' Mac agreed. 'So, what are you going to do now?'

'I'm going to talk to Cathy and tell her everything. That's what I should have done when I first found out. The only thing is though Mac...'

From Johnny's pleading look he knew that the rock star was going to ask him a favour.

'Okay, what is it?' Mac asked.

'Could you go in and kind of calm her down a bit first. I know Cathy and, if I poke my head around the door, she'll throw something at me.'

Mac thought about this for a few seconds and then sighed. He could see Johnny's predicament having already heard about Cathy Conyers' temper.

'Okay,' he replied with a sigh.

He sincerely hoped that Cathy would restrain herself when he told her what he was there for.

Mac asked Kate to pull over when they were not too far from the hotel and Johnny got back into the boot. The press were waiting for them as they drove into the car park and several well-muscled security men were just about keeping them at bay.

To the astonishment of some guests who were just leaving the hotel Johnny climbed out of the boot and straightened himself up.

'As you can see it's not all fun being famous,' Johnny said to Kate. He turned to Mac and, looking more than a bit nervous, said, 'Here we go then. Say a little prayer for me, Mac.'

In the hallway outside of Cathy's hotel room Mac whispered to Johnny that he should stay put and out of sight until he came out again. Mac hesitated for a moment while he got it clear in his head exactly what he was going to say to Cathy before knocking at the door. She opened the door and, seeing who it was, she managed a half smile while she held the door open for him.

'Back again so soon, Mr. Maguire. I take it that you have some news for me then?' Cathy said.

Mac thought that she looked quite apprehensive. He could well understand that. Whatever news she'd had recently had been all bad.

'Yes, I suppose I do have some news, news to you at least.'

Mac had decided to keep it simple and be honest and, if the worst came to the worst, use his crutch to ward off any flying objects.

'I've got Johnny waiting in the hallway outside. He needs to speak to you.'

He could see the anger immediately flare up in her eyes.

'Get out!' she said loudly. 'I don't know what you think you're up to but just get out.'

'Cathy please, it's important that you see him and that you listen to what he says. Look, I know that you've been in a lot of pain after splitting up with him, and you still are I'd guess, but it's not what you think. I've heard what Johnny is going to tell you and believe me you're going to want to hear it too. Please trust me and give Johnny five minutes. That's all it's going to take. Please, just five minutes,' Mac pleaded.

She paced up and down for the next minute or so glancing at Mac from time to time. He could see that she was having a conversation with herself. She stopped and looked at the clock on the wall before turning towards Mac.

'Tell Johnny his five minutes starts now.'

Mac went to the door as quickly as he could and shouted Johnny's name. He appeared from around a corner.

'Did she agree?' he asked his face creased with worry.

'You've got five minutes so get yourself in here quick,' Mac said urgently.

'Please stay with me Mac,' Johnny said his expression showing his desperation all too well.

Mac followed him in.

Cathy turned and, on seeing Johnny, her expression hardened. Johnny tried to smile.

'Hello babs,' he said lamely.

'Johnny, forget the niceties. Mr. Maguire tells me that you've got something to say to me, so say it and get out.'

'Can we at least sit down while I talk?' Johnny asked.

Cathy nodded towards the sofa. She sat in the armchair opposite.

'So, where do I start?' Johnny said almost to himself.

'Why not start with her?' Cathy shouted angrily as she threw a newspaper at her ex-husband.

Johnny picked the paper up from the floor. It was open at a full-page photograph of him and the young woman.

'Yes, we should start with her,' Johnny said quietly.

'Do you love her Johnny?' Cathy asked in a quiet voice.

Mac guessed that it was the one question that Cathy had to ask but, from her apprehensive expression, Mac also guessed that it was also the one question she didn't really want to hear the answer to.

'I do Cathy, I love her as much as I've ever loved anyone.'

Mac saw the hardness in Cathy's face disappear as it crumpled into a despairing look. Johnny went over to her, fell to his knees and took hold of her hand.

'I love her so much because she's my daughter Cathy, she's my beautiful daughter.'

It took a while for this news to sink in. Eventually her despairing expression was replaced by one that had some hope in it.

'She's your daughter? Is that really true?' she asked in wonder.

'Yes, it's true alright,' Johnny said with a wide smile.

'Tell me about her.'

Mac got up and offered the sofa to Cathy and Johnny. He sat in the newly vacated armchair.

'I'm still pinching myself if I'm honest.' Johnny said. 'About a year ago my solicitor received a letter from a Roisin Kavanagh stating that she was my daughter and it requested that my medical records be released.'

'Why did she want your medical records?' Cathy asked.

'Rosie and her husband want to have kids and they just wanted to be sure that there weren't any genetic skeletons in my cupboard. I asked to see her but her solicitor said she preferred not to be contacted directly.

God, you'd think that most girls who found out that they had a father who was rich and famous would be pleased but not my Rosie. She's quite a serious girl and she's not at all impressed by my money or by the way I treated her mom either, if I'm being honest. Anyway, I found that I really wanted to meet her and so I said that I'd only release the medical records if she agreed to see me in person. She agreed, a bit reluctantly I'd guess, but she agreed.

We first met nearly a year ago and I nearly fainted when I saw her, she was so like her mother Clare. We'd been together for six months or so in the late eighties and I thought she was it, the love of my life, but I buggered it up of course.'

'How?' Cathy asked.

Johnny gave her a sad, shameful look.

'It was identical twins, Cathy. I was still fairly young and full of juice and I just couldn't turn them down. I knew it was wrong but there you go. Anyway, Clare came back unexpectedly and caught the three of us in bed. She just gave me this long look of disappointment and left and that was the last I saw of her. I didn't know it but she was pregnant at the time. Anyway, life went on, more records, more tours and then, when I was just about to give up on ever meeting anyone special again, I met you and that was just about the best day of my life. You told me before we married that you couldn't have children and that was okay, I was happy with that.'

Mac saw a look of deep sadness pass over Cathy's face when Johnny said this.

He continued, 'So Rosie and me met and I have to admit that it opened up some really strange locked away feelings. It's hard to explain but, knowing that I had a child in the world made all the difference some-how, like my life wasn't so bloody pointless after all.'

Cathy's put her hand on top of Johnny's and gave it a squeeze. Johnny gave her a smile.

'So, we met and Rosie was quite defensive at first. She hadn't known I was her dad until her mum died five years before. She'd never tried to contact me once in nearly four years until she finally felt that she had to. To be honest, I think that she was a bit ashamed of me, a dad who bites off snake's heads for a living. I honestly think that she'd have preferred it if I'd been a dustman.'

'What does she do?' Cathy asked.

'She's a teacher,' Johnny said proudly. 'A remedial teacher, so is her husband. They try to get kids who have fallen behind with their subjects and bring them up to the same standard as the rest. It's bloody hard graft though. She works mostly with poor kids from some of the roughest parts of London. She took me to where she teaches once, a right shithole it was, and that's where I had my big idea. Why not take the kids right away from their normal surroundings for a while and show them something different? I told her that she could have that mausoleum in St. Albans if she wanted. It's big enough for a school and even for parents to stop overnight if they wanted to. I must admit that the fact it would also keep her close by played a big part in that decision.

Those two days she stayed with me were all about planning for the school. We formed a charity named after her mum and we've signed contracts with the London Boroughs. They'll supply and pay the teachers and the learning materials while the charity pays for the building and all the running costs. That photo was taken when Rosie and I left the party after the gig at the Albert Hall. It was all in support of the school and we used it to launch the charity. Some of my mates were good enough to join in and we made quite a bit.'

'You look like you were getting on well with her in that photo,' Cathy said.

Johnny smiled, 'I think she's warming to me, her husband too. He's a really good bloke even if he does support Chelsea. Anyway, we talked it over with the publicists and we were going to announce it at a press conference next week, to try and get even more publicity for the charity.'

'And you're absolutely sure that she's your daughter? I take it that you've had the DNA tests done?' Cathy asked.

Johnny nodded, 'I didn't need any tests, one look at her was enough for me. I'm afraid Rosie was the one who insisted on the tests. I'm not totally sure if she wasn't disappointed but yes, she's definitely my daughter. She's a gift from whoever's up there,' he said pointing upwards.

'Why in God's name didn't you tell me though?' Cathy asked with some feeling.

'Rosie asked me to promise not to tell anyone and so I didn't, not even you. I'm sorry babs but I was so scared of frightening her away. She's going to have kids some-day, my grandchildren, no our grandchildren, Cathy,' Johnny said giving her hand a little squeeze. 'I want to know them, to see them grow up, to be a real part of their lives. I've seen that sad expression on your face when you look at children all too often and I know how much you would have liked to have one of your own. Well, that's not possible but we could have some grandchildren though. What do you think?'

'What do I think?' Cathy replied as though she was asking the question of herself. Finally, a smile lit up her face as she said, 'I think I'd love to be a grandmother. I also think that we've wasted six months and we've got a hell of a lot of catching up to do.'

Johnny gave her an adoring look and they fell into each other's arms.

Mac made as quick and as quiet an exit as he could. However, he felt that, if a brass band had walked in at that moment, it wouldn't have distracted the two lovers one little bit. He was about to close the door behind him when he had a thought. He reached around the door and took the hanger from the doorknob. He shut the door and put the 'Do not disturb' sign on display. He thought they might be best left alone for a time while they 'caught up'.

Kate could see from Mac's wide smile that things had gone well.

'So, I take it that they're back together again?' she asked.

'Yes, I think you could very safely say that.'

'Good,' Kate said with a smile. 'It's nice to think that things can work out for a change. So where are we off to now?'

Mac looked at his watch. It was still only two o'clock.

'Welwyn, I think. We need to go and see Bill Simmonds, the landlord of the Apple Tree pub. That's where Jimmy and Ben first met each other. I'm hoping that he might be able to tell us something.'

'Do you think he was serious?' Kate asked.

'About his daughter, yes, absolutely,' Mac replied.

'No, I meant about the video.'

'What I've learnt about Johnny so far is that he's just a straightforward type of person, one who doesn't seem to go in for sarcasm or irony all that much. So, if I were you, I'd start thinking about what I was going to wear for the video shoot.'

Kate gave him a worried glance.

The pub, for all that it stood in a nondescript housing estate, looked quite impressive with its peaked roof and rows of white edged windows. At this time of day, the pub was nearly empty and thankfully it was also quite cool inside. Mac ordered two sparkling waters for himself and Kate. He also asked for the landlord.

They sat at a nearby table and waited. For some reason Tim's suggestion to 'follow the money' kept popping up in his head but he had no idea why.

'So, what do you think we'll learn from the landlord?' Kate asked.

Mac shrugged.

'I've no idea but if Ben drank here regularly then I'd bet that Bill Simmonds will know quite a lot about him. I've found that pub landlords are usually a good source of information. Their customers always say more than they might normally once they've had a few drinks inside them.'

Ten minutes later a man in his late thirties sat down opposite them. He was thin and sweating from some exertion. He had a tracksuit and trainers on but, unlike many of his customers, Mac guessed that he knew how to use them.

'You run?' Mac asked.

'Yes, five miles every day. I'm Bill Simmonds. I hear that you've been asking for me.'

Mac showed him his warrant card.

'How can I help the police?' he asked.

'I take it that you've heard about Ben Meeks?'

'Yes, it was on the news this morning. I must admit that I was quite shocked. You never think that things like that will happen to someone you know, do you?'

'We're trying to get some background information on Ben. Anything that might help us to find his killer,' Mac asked.

'I'm not sure I can really tell you that much. Ben used to come in here a couple of times a week I suppose. It used to be a lot more before he went to work for that actress. He was always a bit of a lad, always up for a laugh. On his day off he used to spend most of the day here, especially if there was racing on.'

'He liked the horses then?'

'He loved them. He always had a racing paper on him,' the landlord said. 'He used to nip out to the bookies down the road to lay his bets until a few months ago. Then he started using his phone to lay bets.'

'Why was that?' Mac asked although he had an idea.

'I'm not sure but I did hear from someone that he'd used up his credit limit at more than one of the local bookies. I'm not sure if that's true as he certainly seemed to be okay for money lately.'

'Is there anything else that you can tell me?'

Bill shrugged.

'Not really. I don't remember seeing him with anyone in particular lately, except for Jimmy.'

'Thanks anyway.' Mac got up to leave and then asked, 'How do I get to the bookies from here?'

'Just turn left when you leave the pub, it's only a couple of hundred yards up on the same side of the street.'

Although it wasn't that far away Mac took no chances. He got Kate to drive down in the car and park as close as she could. The bookie's shop was even emptier than the pub with just the one punter gazing disinterestedly up at a race on one of the monitors. At the rear of the shop a middle-aged woman sat behind a high counter. She was doing word puzzles and was obviously bored to tears.

'Excuse me,' Mac said. 'Can I see the manager?'

'You're looking at her,' she replied without looking up.

Mac placed his warrant card on top of the puzzle book and she looked up at him.

'Did you know Ben Meeks?'

'Yes, I heard all about his murder this morning. A dreadful thing that was,' she said with a sad look. 'He was such a fit young man as well. So, how can I help?'

'We're looking for some background information, anything at all that you can tell us about Ben.'

'Well, he loved the horses,' she said. 'It was just a pity he was so useless at picking winners. A pity for him, I mean, it was good business for me.'

'I heard that he had some money problems,' Mac said fishing for a response.

'Well, as cute as he was, I didn't allow him much of a credit limit. We're only a small business. However, he did come around here three or four weeks ago begging me to extend his credit limit.'

'And did you?'

She shook her head.

'I heard later on that he'd managed to get some credit with Barry Cruthers. He runs a couple of shops in Hitchin.' She looked right and left before lowering her voice, 'I heard that he was into Barry for over ten thousand and that Barry had his boys out looking for him.'

'What happened?' Mac asked.

'Well, fortunately for Ben he came into some money, although God knows where from. Anyway, he was suddenly flush and he didn't need any credit. I heard that he paid back Barry with a bit on top and that's how come he kept his good looks. He laid a big bet here only a couple of days ago on a race and guess what? The horse only won. That's rich, isn't it?' she said as she shook her head.

Mac was able to get Barry Cruthers' phone number from the manager and called him as they drove towards Hitchin. Barry answered and Mac arranged to meet him in his shop. This shop was quite a bit busier. At least ten punters were transfixed as they looked at a race on the numerous TVs scattered around the shop. Barry waved at Mac and Kate and took them into a small back room containing boxes of blank betting slips and short pencils. Barry was in his late forties, of stocky build and his nose and ears showed the wear and tear of a long boxing career. He reminded Mac of a bulldog for some reason.

Mac showed him his warrant card which Barry read carefully.

'I thought so. You're that ex-copper, the one who used to be in the murder squad,' he stated as he handed the card back.

'I'm working with the police at the moment and I'm trying to find out as much as I can about Ben Meeks.'

'That little shit! When I heard that it was him that was killed, I must admit that I didn't shed a tear.'

'Why was that?' Mac asked.

'He gave me some spiel a while back about how he was putting bets on for his boss, not himself. He told me that she couldn't afford the publicity and all that. He was plausible alright and, me being the trusting kind, I gave him some credit which he soon used up. I found out later that I wasn't the only one he'd told that bare-faced lie to. Then he got quite hard to find until a couple of my boys caught him behind the wheel of that big Bentley he drove. He was more like a jellyfish than a man when they escorted him back here. They hadn't laid a finger on him but he was blubbering and swearing blind he was good for the money. I gave him one last chance and said that if he didn't have the money in a week, well...'

'I take it that he came up with it then?' Mac asked.

Barry nodded, 'I must admit that really surprised me. He even came up with twenty per cent on top as a sweetener. It saved his bacon as me and the boys were going to get bit physical with him, if you know what I mean.'

Mac knew all too well what the bookie meant.

'Did he say how he came by the money?'

'He said that his aunt had died and left it to him. It was handy that. If I was you, I'd check that he didn't do his aunt in for her money.'

Mac also thought that might be a good idea.

'From what you've said, I take it that you didn't think much of Ben Meeks.'

'In my business you meet all types,' Barry said. 'I've had people owe me money before but, if they're men about it and take their punishment, I don't hold it against them. But Ben, he was the slippery type; always excuses, always lies and he was a bloody coward too. When we had our little chat, he almost pissed himself.'

'So, what happened when he paid the money back?'

'I told him that, if he ever entered any of my shops again, I'd break his arms and legs for him,' Barry replied. 'I haven't seen him since.'

Mac wasn't altogether surprised about that.

'Do you know if he paid back the other bookies that he owed money to?'

'That's what I heard. It must have come to well over twenty grand in all, I reckon.'

Outside Mac stood on the pavement thinking about what he'd learnt about Ben Meeks. He'd recklessly run up big debts and had then somehow come into enough money to pay them back. Barry Cruthers had described Ben as 'slippery' and Mac had some respect for the opinions of bookies. They tended to know human nature all too well.

'So, Ben gets twenty thousand from somewhere then a few weeks later there's a robbery and it looks like an inside job. A coincidence, do you think?' Kate asked.

'I doubt it and I think I now know why Ben was so keen to get Jimmy the job with Cathy Conyers,' Mac said.

The idea that had popped into his head while talking to Cathy Conyers had now gained some traction with Mac. He looked at his watch. It was just past four. He was going to do as Tim suggested and follow the money.

Chapter Eleven

Mac rang Dan and let him know that he was on his way back to the incident room. The press were still out in full force and they had to undergo a barrage of camera flashes on their way in. One or two in the press scrum had obviously done their research and they recognised him. They started shouting questions at the car.

'DCS Maguire, why have they brought you in?'

'We've heard that the police don't know what they're doing? Is that true?'

'What are they hiding, Mr. Maguire?'

'Was it Cathy or Johnny who killed the chauffeur?'

Mac did his best not to react in any way and he was relieved when the policemen finally let them through the cordon.

Dan seemed glad to see them and he ushered him and Kate straight into an interview room.

'I see that the press found out that I'm involved,' Mac said.

'They're a bloody nuisance but it's only to be expected considering who's involved in this case,' Dan replied. 'Someone in the papers called the case Britain's best reality TV show, if you can believe that. Anyway, I hope that you've got something as my boss is going ballistic. He's coming under all sorts of pressure and I'm afraid that he's passing most of it on to me.'

'Yes, I think that we might have. Tell me what have you found out about Ben Meeks so far?' Mac asked.

'Well, he's never been involved with us before, in fact the only thing we could find on him was some out-standing parking tickets for that Bentley he drove. Miss Conyers said that he was a good worker and that she trusted him. He had no close friends as far as we're aware and that's about it really,' Dan said with a shrug.

'It's not much I know but we've been concentrating on finding out as much as we could about Jimmy.'

Mac told Dan what he'd discovered.

'Did you manage to get a look at Ben's bank account?' Mac asked.

'Yes, there was nothing out of the ordinary, just his pay going in. Although I did notice that he hadn't spent much of it in the last two weeks or so.'

'What about his aunt in Salford?' Mac asked. 'He told one of the bookies that she'd died and left him the money.'

'Well, this morning she was alive and living in a council estate,' Dan said. 'I spoke to the detective in Salford who interviewed her myself. She's disabled and on benefits. I doubt that she has two pound coins to rub together at the moment, never mind twenty thousand. The story is that Ben Meeks was in a relationship with a girl in Salford and that he then got her pregnant. So, he did a runner to Welwyn just after he got the news and he somehow forgot to leave the girl a forwarding address. Apparently, her family are strict Christians, so Christian in fact that they threw her out when she told them that she was pregnant. She and her baby are now living with the aunt. She's working and, with the aunt's benefits, they get by. From what the detective told me, if this girl had known where he lived then she'd be a good suspect for his murder.'

'That says a lot about Ben's character, doesn't it?' Mac said. 'Okay, so Ben suddenly gets a lot of money from somewhere. It's more than enough to pay all his debts and in cash too. Then the painting is stolen. Does that suggest anything to you?'

'Yes, it does. It suggests that we might be going after the wrong man.' Dan was thoughtful for a while. 'Okay, this new information is certainly starting to put Ben Meeks into the frame but it's still not enough. All we have is that he suddenly came into a large sum of money.

We need to find out where it came from. It certainly looks dodgy but, for all we know, he might have won the lottery or something. Basically, we've got a squeaky-clean dead chauffeur on one hand while on the other I've got a convicted criminal with some clear circumstantial evidence against him. However, apart from the evidence we found in the shed, we've not been able to find a single thing against Jimmy Carmichael, not even a parking ticket. The problem is that my boss likes him for it and he wants this wrapped up within the next half hour if at all possible. You can see the spot I'm in.'

Mac could. He'd been in similar situations himself.

'So, what would it need to convince your boss to start looking seriously at Ben Meeks as a possible accomplice?' Mac asked.

'We'd need something more than just the money if I'm to let Jimmy Carmichael go.' Mac looked sharply at Dan. 'Yes, I'll admit that I have started to come around to your way of thinking. I've had a look at some of Jimmy's alleged handiwork and he is good. I have to admit that you were right, there's no way I could see him leaving incriminating evidence lying around like that. However, I need something more substantial that I can show my boss before we can let Jimmy go free.'

'Thanks Dan. I'll do my level best to get it for you.'

Mac left feeling a whole lot better than when he went in. He said his goodbyes to Kate and, on his way back to the car, he rang Tim and arranged to meet him in the Magnets.

'Mac?'

It was Kate. Mac turned and looked at her.

'Would you mind if I come along with you?' she asked. 'I know you're meeting your friend so if you don't want me to...'

Mac didn't reply. He just went around to the passenger side of his car, smiled and held the door open for her. The car was surrounded by the press as he drove out of the car park and he was nearly blinded by the camera flashes. Once again questions were shouted at Mac and, once again, he studiously ignored them.

'I take it that you can catch the train to the station in the morning?' Mac asked as they drove down the road.

'Yes, I usually do when I'm working in Letchworth. I'll get a taxi to the incident room tomorrow.'

'Don't worry about that. I'll pick you up at the station, just ring me ten minutes before you get in.'

Kate turned and looked at Mac with real gratitude.

'Thanks Mac, I really appreciate it.'

'It's nothing, we're a team now.'

As they drove Mac kept looking in the mirror in case any of the press had decided to follow them. One car did seem to be doing just that but he lost them by over-taking a slow lorry on the narrow country road. Then, once out of sight of the following car, he pulled into the drive of a private house that had a high hedge in front and parked up for a few minutes. He saw the curtain twitching and a disapproving face appear at the window. He smiled and gave them a wave before reversing the car and driving out again.

It was nearly seven by the time he was once again seated in his favourite pub. Tim had managed to get their usual table, number thirteen next to one of the large plate glass windows. Mac had always enjoyed looking out at the comings and goings on the high street so Tim was clearly puzzled when Mac waved towards a table situated right at the back of the pub.

'If the press spot me then it might mean an abrupt end to our night out. So, it might be best to keep ourselves well out of view. By the way this is Kate. We're working together on the case,' Mac explained.

Tim was obviously surprised at finding out that Kate was with Mac. He gave Mac a very meaningful wink which made him smile. Tim did the honourable thing and went to the bar while Mac sat and talked to his colleague.

'I'm sorry about imposing on you and your friend but I just didn't want to go straight home tonight,' Kate said.

Mac felt for Kate. He knew from experience that it was no fun going home to an empty house when you're feeling a bit low.

'That's okay, I usually have a chat with Tim about whatever case I'm working on anyway. To be honest, I've had some of my best ideas about cases in pubs,' Mac said. 'Unfortunately, we also tend to talk a lot about football too.'

'Why is that unfortunate?' Kate asked.

'You're a football fan then?'

'You bet. I used to play too, until I got married that is.'

'My apologies Kate. I think that I just made an unwarranted assumption there. Who do you support?' Mac asked.

'Barnet.'

'Barnet? They're in League Two, aren't they?'

'Yes, but only just. We used to live not far away from the ground and I started going to matches to keep my little brother company as my father was always too busy. I ended up getting hooked myself.'

'Who did you play for?' Mac asked.

'The London Bees, that's the Barnet women's team. I was a creative mid-fielder or at least I tried to be.'

Their conversation was interrupted by the arrival of the drinks. Tim handed Mac a welcome pint of lager and Kate a large red wine.

'Now, you might be surprised to know that Kate here has some hidden depths,' Mac said to Tim. 'Did you know that you're looking at Barnet's answer to Andres Iniesta?'

Tim gave Mac a surprised look while Kate just looked embarrassed. Mac told him what he'd just learnt.

110

'Tell me did you ever get to meet Edgar Davids?' Tim asked with some excitement.

Mac knew that Tim had been a fan of Davids ever since he'd seen him play alongside Zidane for Juventus in Turin some years before.

'I saw him there a few times but, sadly, I never got to meet him properly,' Kate explained.

'I'm not sure whether Mac's told you yet but we're supporters of a club called Aston Villa. They've got a great history but unfortunately a rubbish team at the moment. Tell me, did you see that United game last Saturday? What did you think about that sending off?' Tim asked.

This led to an evening's debate on the finer points of football, both domestic and European. Mac and Tim knew each other's points of view all too well so it was refreshing to have someone else's opinion thrown into the mix. Mac could see that Tim was very impressed with Kate's knowledge of the game.

In fact, when Kate got up to go to the toilet Tim said, 'My God Mac, what a woman! You should snap her up straight away but, if you're not interested yourself, then I might give it a go. What do you think?'

Mac could only laugh. He knew that Tim was being very far from serious.

'Why the laughter? So long as I've got my own hair and teeth then I'm still in the game,' Tim said with a wide smile and a glint in his eye that contradicted everything he said.

They got so carried away with their discussion that Kate missed her last train home and Mac persuaded her to come back with him and use the guest room.

As they got the taxi back Kate thanked Mac again.

'Oh, there's no need for thanks. That's the best night that Tim and me have had for ages and we didn't even discuss the case once.'

Mac opened the front door quietly, forgetting for a moment that Bridget and Tommy were on the other side of Europe. Kate sat on the sofa while Mac made coffee. By the time he came back with the coffee she was on her side and fast asleep. Mac took her shoes off and put her legs up on the sofa. He fetched a sheet and a pillow from the guest room and placed the pillow under her head and covered her up with the sheet. He turned off the light and left her to sleep.

While he was brushing his teeth, he thought about Kate. He felt that she was somehow lost and in pain. He was sure about this because he too felt that he was pretty much in the same boat.

He lay down in a bed that was too big for him and turned off the light.

'Good night, Nora,' he said out loud.

He lay on his side and his right arm automatically went over to the other side of the bed. It only embraced emptiness. The pain was bad but for once it had nothing to do with his back.

He had trouble sleeping as the air felt hot and thick and stagnant. The sound of a much-needed thunder-storm in the distance didn't help much at first but then the welcome sounds of raindrops came and, coupled with a fresher feel to the air, it soothed Mac into a deep sleep. Even when the rain became so heavy that the sound of it bashing off the roof and windows should have woken him, Mac slept soundly on.

If anyone could have seen him, they'd have noticed a smile on his face. He was dreaming and, in his dreams, he was once again with his Nora.

Chapter Twelve

Kate awoke in stages. She was trying to remember what had happened the night before but she was having problems. Her hand felt the texture of whatever it was she was lying on. It felt strange. Where was she? The welcome aroma of coffee finally persuaded her to open her eyes. She was in someone's living room. Yes, it was Mac's. She remembered that she'd been talking to Mac and his friend Tim in the pub the evening before. She looked at the clock. It had just gone nine. She jumped up in panic just as Mac came in with a cup of coffee.

'Oh, you're up. Did you sleep well?' Mac asked.

'Too well, it's nine o'clock!' she said anxiously. 'We should be at work.'

'You looked like you needed your sleep but don't worry. I rang Dan and said that we were checking something out and that we'd be in a little later this morning.'

'And what's this something we're supposed to be checking out then?' Kate asked as she sat up and gratefully accepted a steaming mug of coffee.

'Now, that's our first challenge of the day,' Mac said with a smile. 'Anyway, drink your coffee and then I'll do you some breakfast while you have a shower.'

She felt better as she sipped at her coffee. Mac had been right when he'd said that she'd needed her sleep. She hadn't been sleeping well lately. In fact, last night had been the best night that she'd had for some time. She found it strange that she could sleep better on someone's sofa than in her own bed.

After a shower she felt quite awake and was more than ready for the eggs and bacon that Mac put in front of her. She was suddenly hungry and wolfed it down.

'We had quite a thunderstorm last night,' Mac said. 'At least the garden will be all the better for it.'

'Did we? I never heard a thing,' she replied. 'So, have you had any ideas yet?'

Mac fired up his laptop.

'Yes, something did occur to me. It was something Tim said about following the money.'

'Following the money? You mean finding out where Ben Meeks got the cash from?' Kate asked.

'Not necessarily. Tim was referring to a quote from a film about Watergate and how two journalists broke the story. It was a really complex story with leads going in all directions but an informant told them to just 'Follow the money', the money being something physical that they could actually track.'

'Okay, so what's the physical thing that we should be looking for then?' Kate asked.

'The dog. With all that's been going on I've been totally forgetting about Charmaine.'

'If they killed Ben Meeks then wouldn't they have killed the dog too?' Kate asked.

'Not necessarily. I was lying awake this morning trying to figure it out in my head. I was thinking about what Ben Meeks' motives might have been for taking part in the robbery. What do you think they were?' Mac asked.

'The money?' Kate ventured.

'Yes, there was that. The money solved an immediate problem for him but I think there was something else, another inducement that persuaded him to take part in robbing his own boss. Jimmy told me that Ben had really cared for Cathy Conyers in his own way. So, I started wondering if the main reason he went along with the robbery was because he wanted to impress her.'

Kate's face crinkled in thought as she took on board what Mac had said.

'So, you think that Ben might have wanted to play the hero but his accomplice had other ideas? Is that it?' she asked.

'That's exactly it,' Mac replied. 'The plan, as far as Ben might have been aware, was for him to first get the information on the alarm system. In the meantime, his accomplice was out knocking over the cook's sister. So, with the cook safely out of the way, there would only be Ben in the house. Once Ben had let him in, the accomplice would disable the security system and take the painting. He would then rough Ben up a little. Enough anyway to make it look like he did his best to stop the theft.'

'So, he then looks like a hero to Cathy Conyers,' Kate said. 'Yes, I get that but what about the dog then?'

'I'm thinking that it might have been another chance for Ben to play the hero and that he might have put Charmaine somewhere in the hope that he could go back and get her later. He would then triumphantly bring her back to Miss Conyers who would fall into his arms and they'd live happily ever after.'

'It's all a bit simplistic though, isn't it?' Kate said her face showing her scepticism.

'To you and me perhaps but I think that Ben might have just been gullible enough to believe that something like that might be possible. It was Ben who suggested the idea and then arranged for Eleanor Tarbridge, Cathy's assistant, to be away on a cruise. From what he said, I gathered that nothing much was likely to happen between him and Cathy while her assistant was around. I also think that his accomplice might have played on this too, not just the money but Miss Conyers and the gravy train for life.'

'Okay, I agree that it's worth following up but how?' Kate asked.

'Here,' Mac said pointing to his laptop.

Mac was on Google Earth and the screen showed the countryside in the vicinity around Cathy Conyers' house.

'So, what are we looking for exactly?' Kate asked.

'Any isolated outhouses or barns in the area that aren't too far from a public road. Somewhere a dog could be safely kept out of the way for a number of days.'

On the screen he followed the lane outside the house in both directions, then down any side roads in roughly a five-mile radius. Using the satellite view they found six candidates in all and Mac printed off a map for each one. The maps showed the co-ordinates for each of the outhouses, allowing Mac to insert them into his satnav to ensure that they'd go to exactly the right location.

Kate frowned as she watched Mac fill up an empty milk container with water.

'If Ben Meeks was keeping the dog, it will have been cooped up somewhere for a few days now. With the weather having been so warm recently do you really think there's much chance of finding her alive?' she asked.

Mac returned the frown.

'Probably not but you never know.'

Just in case Mac stopped and picked up some supplies at a local shop before they made their way towards Shaw's Corner.

The first two outhouses were obviously derelict, falling down and unfortunately empty. The third, down the end of a long marshy lane, was clearly in use as a suspicious farmer was getting some complicated machinery from the small barn and hitching it up to a tractor. He glowered at Mac and Kate as the old Almera struggled to make a U turn in two feet of mud. Mac could still feel his hot glare on his back as he finally succeeded in turning the car around and slowly drove away.

'Welcoming sort, wasn't he?' Kate said dryly.

The fourth one looked a bit more promising. Mac stopped and looked at the map on the satnav.

'The outhouse is just around that corner. I think we should leave the car where it is just in case there might be any tyre tracks,' Mac said.

Kate looked at the dirt road. Last night's storm had turned it into a muddy quagmire.

'Do you really think there'll be any tracks left after last night's rain?' she asked.

'Probably not but it's still better to be on the safe side.'

Mac noticed Kate looking out at the muddy morass outside and then down at her highly inadequate and fragile looking sling back shoes.

'What shoe size are you?' Mac asked.

'Six.'

'Well, they'll be a bit big but I do have some wellies in the boot.'

She smiled, 'Thanks Mac. These wouldn't last a second.'

He took the bottle of water and a plastic bag from the boot and handed Kate a pair of black size ten wellington boots. He had to admit that she looked quite comical in them.

Mac gingerly walked around the corner looking from side to side for any tyre tracks. Kate followed in his footsteps. As they rounded the corner Mac could see a large metal shed standing some fifty yards away. It seemed to be in reasonable condition but it was clearly not in regular use anymore. Weeds had grown up around the door and it had a forlorn look of neglect about it. At the front of the shed there was a sort of covered porch big enough to allow a vehicle to be loaded out of the rain. Beneath this a set of tyre tracks could be clearly seen on the ground. Luckily the roof had protected the tracks from being washed away by the rain.

'Well, someone's been here,' Mac said pointing at the tracks.

He stopped and looked around. He was sure that this must be the place. It was just a short drive from Cathy

Conyers' house while still being well off the beaten track. He hesitated before opening the door. He'd brought water and food along but he wasn't at all hopeful.

He sighed. Charmaine was only a dog but it would still be another death. There was a deep silence as he pulled a paper handkerchief from his pocket and his hand went towards the door. Mac could only fear the worst.

The metal door screeched as he pulled it open and Mac heard a sound that was absolute music to his ears. Charmaine was chained up in a corner and she was barking furiously. Two empty metal bowls were on the ground before her. She must have been there for some time and Mac was not only surprised that she was in such good condition but that she was alive at all given how hot the weather had been.

He guessed that Ben had left her some water and food in the bowls but then he'd expected he'd be alive and that he'd be able to release her before it ran out. However, Charmaine had been lucky. A hole in the roof had caused a puddle of water to collect in a large hollow in the floor. He guessed that if it hadn't had been for that she'd have been dead by now.

'Are you any good with dogs?' Mac asked Kate hopefully.

She shook her head with certainty.

Mac sighed. Charmaine was still barking furiously and he had to agree with Ben. She was a big dog.

'Oh well, here goes,' Mac said trying to sound more optimistic that he felt.

He took a bowl out of the plastic bag he'd been carrying and filled it from the water bottle. He placed it in front of Charmaine at arm's length. He was no dog expert and so he wasn't sure what sort of mood Charmaine might be in after being left alone for so long. The dog dived into the water bowl, lapping at it furiously and sending water spraying in all directions.

118

Mac slowly approached her and held his hand out. She gave it a couple of grateful wet licks and then went back to the water bowl. He opened a can of dog food and placed it in the other bowl and Charmaine proceeded to wolf it down. When she'd finished, she jumped up onto her hind legs and, with one foreleg on each shoulder, gave his ear a good licking. Mac found he didn't mind this at all.

'See,' he said to Kate with some relief, 'no problem at all.'

Mac refilled the bowls with more water and dog food and then rang Dan to let him know what they'd found.

'He's on his way,' Mac said, 'and there'll be a forensics team not far behind him. I've also asked him to bring a vet to check Charmaine over just in case. Oh, and his wellies of course.'

They waited by Mac's car until they heard the sound of a car approaching. It pulled up behind Mac's car and a beaming Dan Carter got out closely followed by Andy Reid. He noticed that they were both wearing wellingtons as advised.

'So, what have you got for us Mac?' Dan asked.

Charmaine started barking at hearing new voices outside.

'Well, a dog as you can probably hear but, even more importantly, the forensic evidence that I'm hoping will put Ben Meeks clearly in the frame,' Mac said as they walked towards the shed. 'Look here.'

Mac pointed at the tyre tracks.

'I'm surprised that they survived the storm last night,' Andy said.

'Yes, me too but I'd guess that the direction that the wind was blowing left this porch somewhat sheltered.'

'The Bentley's tyres?' Dan asked.

'That's what I'm thinking,' Mac replied. 'Did forensics mention anything about dog hair in the car boot?'

Dan gave this some thought.

'Yes, they found a blanket covered in dog hairs if I remember right. I'd guess that they assumed that it was used to cover the seat when the dog was in the car.'

Mac thought back to his first drive in the Bentley and how Ben had to remove the cover from the seat.

'They didn't use a blanket. The dog always sat in the front passenger seat and they had a special cover that they used for that.'

'Okay, so that would be consistent with Ben placing the dog in the boot after tranquilising it,' Dan said. 'If those tracks are from the Bentley and we get some finger-prints then I'd guess that might be more than enough to get Jimmy off the hook.'

Mac crossed his fingers and said a little prayer.

'While we're waiting why don't you tell us what you think happened?' Dan asked.

Mac thought for a moment.

'Well, I'm not sure of all the details but I'd be surprised if it hadn't gone something like this. Ben Meeks was in desperate money trouble and, being a somewhat reckless person, he chose a reckless solution. He started doubling the size of his bets in order to try and win enough to pay back what he owed. Unfortunately, he wasn't very good at picking winners, which is what had gotten him into trouble in the first place. So, his debts just kept getting bigger and bigger. It had gotten to the point that at least one bookie was looking to take it out on him physically if he didn't pay up.'

'Why didn't he just do a runner?' Andy asked.

'A good question, after all he'd done just that once before when things had started going wrong for him in Salford. However, I think he really was in love with Cathy Conyers in his own way and I also think this also explains what he did next. When Johnny Kinsella got his marching orders, Ben thought that this was his big chance. The only problem for him was that Cathy didn't see it in the same way. He was just a chauffeur to her. My guess is that he started thinking that he needed to do something dramatic to show himself to her in a new light. I guess that he saw the solution to both problems when his accomplice approached him about stealing the painting.'

'So, you think that it was Ben's job to get rid of the dog?' Dan asked.

'I do,' Mac replied. 'Even though it was a few days before the robbery was due to take place Ben saw the opportunity to get Charmaine out of the way when Johnny Kinsella turned up. Johnny was known for parking so that the electric gate couldn't close properly. Cathy Conyers would be all too willing to believe that Johnny had taken the dog but Ben could also claim that the dog might have escaped through the open gate. If indeed it was ever really left open. Either way it gave a genuine excuse for the dog to be missing without throwing any blame in his direction.

I think it was the accomplice's job to knock down the cook's sister, so getting her out of the way for a while. Ben's other job was to get as much information on the security system so it would look like a genuine break in. Of course, either he or his accomplice knew that we'd eventually figure out that it might be an inside job, so they needed someone who worked there to take the blame for the robbery. It was really handy for Ben that he'd gotten Jimmy Carmichael the job as gardener by conveniently not telling Cathy Conyers about Jimmy's record. Of course, his reasons for doing this at the time might have been to help Jimmy but, when it suited him, I think that he was willing to turn on his friend. And so, he planted the incriminating evidence in the shed betting that, with his record, Jimmy would be the obvious suspect. Of course, he also planned on being alive so he could give evidence as well. I don't think that he'd have had any compunction about sending an innocent man to jail so long as he'd have gotten what he wanted.'

Dan gave this some thought.

121

'So, you think it was the accomplice who killed him then?'

'I think a big part of the deal was Ben wanting to be the hero to impress Cathy Conyers,' Mac said. 'I dare say the plan was for Ben's accomplice to rough him up enough to make it look genuine. Then Ben would testify that it was Jimmy who'd beaten him up and then stolen the painting. That was Ben's plan but I dare say that his accomplice had other ideas. Only Ben knew the thief's identity, so killing Ben would remove the real risk that he would talk at some point and link him to the robbery. I'd guess that he also encouraged Ben to incriminate Jimmy. It would be even better if Jimmy was arrested for the theft as we wouldn't even be looking at Ben and so the accomplice would be even safer.'

'So, Ben Meeks might have brought it all on himself then,' Dan stated.

'Yes, I think that he was probably one of those reckless people who attract trouble and then look for the easy way out,' Mac said. 'Of course, the thief is probably a few countries away by now and thinking he's a whole lot richer too.'

'Well, he's going to be in for a shock then, isn't he?' Dan said with a grim smile.

They were interrupted by the arrival of the forensics van. They immediately busied themselves working on the tyre tracks and looking for any fingerprints while they waited for the vet to arrive. Charmaine was barking non-stop now and Mac was glad when the vet finally arrived some ten minutes later. He went inside the shed and the barking stopped for a few minutes. Five minutes later he came out. From his smile Mac guessed that it wasn't bad news.

'She's slightly dehydrated still but in remarkably good condition considering the weather we've been having,' the vet said. 'She'll be okay to go home as soon as you like.'

122

One of the forensics team asked the vet to accompany him while they took some samples from the dog. The vet came out with Charmaine on a lead and handed him over to Dan who then gave the lead to Andy. Dan had a chat with the forensics team leader before returning.

'We might as well take Charmaine back to Cathy Conyers ourselves as I've got a few questions that I'd like to ask her anyway,' Dan said before turning to Kate. 'Can you hang around and let me know as soon as they find anything?'

'Yes sure,' Kate replied.

Mac got a roll of kitchen towel from the boot of his car and tried to wipe the mud off his shoes and then Charmaine's paws as best he could. Andy opened the back door of the police car and Charmaine jumped in without hesitation.

However, she wasn't content with sitting in the back and, by the time Andy had opened the driver's side door, he found that she was sitting on the front passenger seat. She looked from Andy to the windscreen several times as though saying, 'Why aren't we going yet?'

Mac laughed out loud.

'Dan, I think we'll both have to sit in the back for now.'

Chapter Thirteen

Charmaine was very well behaved as they drove back to the hotel. She sat there with her tongue hanging out and her head constantly going from side to side as she watched the world go by. Of course, the press were still waiting outside and a few desultory flashes went off as they drove towards the car park. They walked Charmaine into the hotel and then headed towards Cathy Conyers' room. The receptionist gave them a look of astonishment as they walked by. Dan tried to ignore him but he ran after them.

'What on earth are you doing? We don't allow dogs in this hotel,' the receptionist said with real feeling as he blocked their path.

Dan stopped, showed him his warrant card and gave him his sternest look.

'This isn't a dog. This is a witness to a murder.'

He didn't explain any further and left a worried and perplexed looking man behind in his wake.

Johnny answered the door. It appeared that he and Cathy had truly kissed and made up.

'Bloody hell, Sharmy!' he exclaimed joyously as he went down on one knee and let the dog wash his face with her tongue.

Cathy's face appeared around the door and, for the first time, Mac saw it lit by a genuine smile.

'It's Charmaine. Oh, thank you!' she said.

The tail was definitely wagging the dog as Charmaine went joyously from Johnny to Cathy and back again. It made Mac smile and for the first time the idea of having a dog himself popped into his head. They had to wait a few minutes for Charmaine to calm down before they could talk.

'Mac tells me that the thief only got away with a copy. Is that true, Miss Conyers?' Dan asked.

'Yes, it's true,' Cathy replied.

'Why didn't you tell us this straight away?'

'Well it was all a bit of a shock and...,'

Cathy stopped and gave them a shame-faced look before she continued.

'No, I'm not going to lie any more. I was ashamed of myself, deeply ashamed. I'd told the lie about that painting so often that I'd almost become to believe it myself. Not even Johnny knew it was a copy.' Johnny came over and held her hand. She looked up at him gratefully. 'Ben died trying to save that painting and I couldn't...I just didn't know what to do.'

Dan's phone rang. He took it out and looked at the screen.

'It's Kate,' he said to Mac and Andy. 'I'm sorry but I'm going to have to take this,' he said to Cathy.

He went into the far corner of the room. All Mac heard was him replying 'Yes' a couple of times. He had half a smile on his face as he came back and Mac knew that forensics had found something.

'Miss Conyers, we're now working on the assumption that Ben Meeks was a party to the robbery which he carried out with an, as yet, unknown accomplice. Mac found your dog but we also found your car's tyre tracks at the spot where Charmaine was being held and Ben Meeks' fingerprints were pretty much all over the place.'

Cathy Conyers looked shocked.

'Ben was in on it? Are you sure?'

'It had to be an inside job. Who else had access to the Bentley?' Dan asked.

'No-one,' Cathy replied. 'Only Ben had the keys and he kept them on him at all times.'

'At some point I may want you to take part in a press conference, if that's okay,' Dan asked. 'We might need to tell the man who killed Ben Meeks exactly what he's stolen.'

'Of course, of course,' she replied looking anxiously at Johnny.

'Don't worry, bab. I'll be there too,' he said.

She smiled as she gripped his hand even tighter.

'Until then, however,' Dan said, 'it's really important that you tell no-one else. Is that understood?'

Cathy nodded.

Dan thanked them both and headed for the door. Mac had been petting Charmaine while Dan spoke and she seemed quite sad to see him go.

Outside Dan turned to Mac and said, 'If you like, you can tell Jimmy that he's a free man yourself.'

'No, I think that it should come from you but I'd like to be there when you do, if that's okay?'

Andy drove them back to the shed. The forensics team were packing up their gear. Dan went over and had a word with them before going back to Mac.

'I just wanted to make sure that they hadn't found any traces belonging to Jimmy. They haven't.'

Mac couldn't blame Dan for being careful. He drove Kate back to the incident room and they had a coffee while they waited. Jimmy arrived in a police car half an hour later.

Jimmy looked composed but determined when they brought him into the interview room. He sat down and nodded to Mac then glowered at Dan. Then his eyes fell on a plastic tray that was placed on the table. Dan shoved the tray closer to Jimmy. It contained all his personal belongings; phone, watch, wallet, belt, comb, keys and loose change. Jimmy looked at both Andy and Mac with a mixture of hope and suspicion.

'You're free to go,' Dan said.

Jimmy didn't seem to quite believe it.

'Why?' he asked clearly puzzled by Dan's words.

Dan told him what they'd discovered about Ben. Jimmy seemed truly shocked.

'I knew he was a bit of a chancer but I never thought he'd…well, betray me like that.'

'We'll be in contact if we need you again but for now go home Jimmy,' Dan said as he stood up. 'I'm sure your family are missing you.'

He held out his hand and Jimmy shook it with conviction.

'Thank you, Mr. Carter.'

'Come on, Jimmy. I'll give you a lift home if you like,' Mac offered.

Before they got in the car Jimmy phoned his wife. When he'd finished, he was grinning from ear to ear.

'Where to?' Mac asked.

Jimmy didn't reply for a moment, he seemed quite stunned.

'Oh, the wife's mother's house. I've left my van there. I honestly didn't think I'd be needing it for quite a while,' he said.

He gave Mac the address.

'Thank you, Mr. Maguire. I know that you played a big part in all this. God, I never want to be inside again. Even a couple of days in a police cell was too much for me.' Jimmy went quiet for a moment. 'I suppose Cathy knows all about me now.'

'She does.'

'So, it's back to square one then, isn't it?' Jimmy said as he gave Mac a dejected look. 'Tomorrow I'll have to start looking for another job again.'

'I wouldn't be too sure about that. Go and see Cathy when she's allowed back home. I'm not a betting man but I'd put some money on you still being her gardener and for some time to come too. She's quite a fan of yours actually.'

Mac had to admit that he'd never seen Jimmy look so pleased.

'I hope you're right. I really love that job. I'll do just as you say.'

Jimmy's wife was waiting outside the house for him.

'Thanks again,' Jimmy said as he got out of the car.

His wife ran towards him and they hugged each other. Mac had a sad moment as he watched them. He hoped that Jimmy knew how truly lucky and blessed he was.

While he was in Welwyn, he thought that he might as well go back to the bookies and collect Ben's winnings. The manager seemed somewhat relieved at Mac's suggestion.

'I really didn't like holding on to that money if I'm honest, it belonging to a dead man and all,' she said as she gave him a cheque for well over a thousand pounds. 'And, from what you've told me, it's going to a good cause anyway.'

She found Mac an envelope and a sheet of paper. It had the bookies heading on it but Mac was sure that the recipient wouldn't mind. In the note he briefly stated that, as she was Ben Meeks' only relative, the money belonged to her and also to the baby he'd left behind. He then put Ben's aunt's address on the envelope. Before he sealed it, he had another thought and pulled out Cathy Conyers' cheque from his wallet. He made that out in the aunt's name and put that in the envelope as well.

At least there'll be a silver lining for somebody, Mac thought.

Before he left, he asked the manager if she'd remembered anything else. He was expecting the usual negative answer and was half turned to go when she surprised him.

'Yes, I did remember something but I'm not sure if it's important or anything.'

'Go on,' Mac prompted.

'Well, my husband's a fireman, a Divisional Officer actually,' she said giving Mac a self-deprecating smile. 'Well, at least one of us is doing something useful. Anyway, with the odd hours he works we don't get to go out that often so, when we do, we like to splash out a bit. About a month or so ago we reserved a table for dinner at the Grange Hall Hotel not expecting to see anyone we knew there but guess what?'

'I take it that Ben was there,' Mac said.

'I only caught a glimpse but it was definitely him. He was tucked away in a corner of the bar with another man.'

'What did you think about seeing him there?'

'I knew that it was a bit too rich for him,' she replied, 'especially with all his money worries. So, I assumed that he must have been there on his boss's business. I thought the other man might be an agent or film producer or something.'

'Did you get a look at the other man?' Mac asked.

'Sorry no, I didn't. He had his back to us.'

'Did you manage to hear anything they said?'

'No, as I say they were quite a distance away and I only caught a glimpse of them as we were on our way into the restaurant. I looked again but, when we came out, they'd gone.'

Mac gave this some thought. Having been to that hotel, he knew how expensive it was. He could buy half of the Magnets a drink for what they charged for a single round there. It was definitely out of a chauffeur's league, especially as the chauffeur in question was stony broke.

'What was Ben's expression like? Was he laughing, happy, sad, serious...what?' Mac asked.

'He definitely wasn't laughing. No...'

She stopped and looked up and off to the left, recreating the scene in her mind.

'I never thought anything of it at the time but I'd say he looked quite serious and possibly even a little scared.'

'This man he was with, is there anything you can tell me about him?' Mac asked.

Again, she looked off to the left.

'Well, he was dark haired and wearing something dark but that's all I could see, I'm afraid.'

'Please think again, are you sure that there's nothing else?'

Unfortunately, she couldn't think of anything to add to her story. Mac got her to confirm the exact date before he left. He then drove back to the incident room.

'So, where are we then Mac?' Dan asked.

'Well, I think we can say with more or less complete certainty that Ben Meeks was involved and it's highly likely that it was his accomplice who murdered him. As to who that might have been, we haven't got a clue,' Mac replied. 'It's time to bring in some help.'

Chapter Fourteen

The morning afterwards Mac was just finishing his second cup of coffee when he heard a key in the door. He'd forgotten that it was one of Amrit's work days. She had a light flowing purple sari on, one that Mac hadn't seen before. He idly wondered just how many saris she owned.

As usual, she sat him down and asked him how his back pain had been since the last time they'd talked. She'd been a pain nurse before she retired and they'd agreed that keeping a pain diary might be a good thing. As Mac had tried it before, and had kept forgetting to update the diary, Amrit decided to do it for him.

'Have you spotted any patterns yet?' he asked.

'No, but we've only just started, haven't we? We'll need to keep it going for at least a few months before we'll see anything concrete. By the way, how's the case going?' she asked excitedly.

'I'm not sure but, if I'm being honest, I've got a feeling that today might just be a crucial day.'

When he arrived at the incident room, he found the team hanging around waiting for the 'help' to come. Dan looked at his watch.

'He did say ten, didn't he?' Dan asked as he looked at his watch again.

It was now two minutes past ten.

'So, you say that you've worked with this Hamish before?' Dan asked.

'Yes, on two cases involving stolen paintings. One from a London museum not long ago and the other from a private home a few years before that,' Mac replied. 'I must admit that he was nothing like I'd expected him to be. I assumed that our top expert from the police Arts and Antiquities section might look more like a professor or something. Anyway, he impressed me. He really knows his stuff.'

While they were waiting Mac had an idea and rang the hotel. He gave the receptionist the exact date that Ben Meeks had been spotted in the hotel. He was lucky as he discovered that a wedding reception had also taken place that same evening. He asked the receptionist if they could send the details and the full guest list to Martin Selby.

'Sorry for the slight delay,' a soft voice said from a very darkened doorway.

Hamish Hamilton dominated the room as he walked in. This was mainly due to him being six foot four and built like the side of a barn. Looking at him you might guess that he played rugby and you'd be right. Some years earlier, he'd played quite a few games for the Scottish international team but, getting into his late thirties now, he only played the occasional game for his club. Hamish was from Glasgow but his voice was soft and had few of the city's strident tones.

Mac shook Hamish's hand and introduced him to Dan and Andy.

'I'm sorry but part of the reason why I'm late was because I've been doing some digging. This is what I've come up with,' Hamish said.

He opened his backpack and pulled out a file. He spread six pictures out on the desk.

'These are the best candidates I've come up with so far with regard to the theft of the Munch. They're all top art thieves and all of them work for cash up front. However, I'd take these three out. For two of them murder hasn't ever been part of their MO while the other one is currently behind bars in St. Petersburg, Russia. That just leaves us with these three.'

Hamish pointed to a picture of man in his late twenties. He had blonde hair and a chubby face.

'The first one is Swedish, Christer Allan Henriksohn, who is twenty-nine years old. We think that he's been responsible for several thefts, including the recent one in Amsterdam where five impressionist paintings worth over ten million went missing. I think it's unlikely that he'd have two jobs planned so close together though. This next one is Luca Russo, he's a Sicilian but we don't think he's Mafia related.'

Hamish held up the photo of a dark-skinned man in his forties with a shaved head.

'He's supposed to have made his money and retired. According to the Italian police he's still living quietly in a place called Catania in Sicily. A possibility perhaps but personally I'd put my money on this one.'

Hamish tapped at the photo of a man in his early thirties with a long face, a hawk-like nose and short dark hair.

'This is Sean Bernard Linville. He's probably the most wanted art thief in Europe but, frustratingly, we've not found any compelling evidence against him as yet. We think that he's the best and also the most ruthless art thief out there. There've been at least three murders related to thefts that we think he's carried out. The first probably wasn't premeditated. We think that Linville was discovered in the act of stealing a painting by a guard who was in an area he hadn't been assigned to. He was new to the job and, unfortunately for him, it looks like he lost his way. The guard died through several very heavy blows to the head with a blunt instrument.'

'Well, that sounds familiar,' Andy commented.

'Yes, he seems to like using a cosh. He used it in the second murder too but there we think that the guard he murdered was an accomplice rather than just an innocent bystander. The third murder was when we found the chief guard of a museum in his burnt-out car. He left a note in the gallery stating that he'd stolen the painting and was intending to commit suicide by setting fire to his car and taking the painting with him. However, the evidence later showed that he too had his head bashed in before he was set on fire, so we know that the note was a fake. Are you still absolutely sure that the painting that was stolen was a copy?'

'Well, Cathy Conyers says it is and the bank has confirmed that they still have a painting in their vault,' Dan said.

'Well, it must have been a bloody good copy if it fooled any of these,' Hamish replied.

'Can I borrow those photos?' Mac asked.

He took them over to Martin and explained his idea. Martin was the team's computer expert and Mac had a lot of respect for his talents. If anyone could do what Mac was asking for then he knew it would be him. Martin confirmed that he'd received the guest list and that it should help narrow things down a bit.

'One of the reasons why we've never been able to pin anything on this Linville is that he always seems to have an alibi,' Mac heard Hamish say as he walked back.

He noticed that Dan was giving him a questioning look.

'We know that Ben Meeks met someone at the Grange Hall Hotel,' Mac explained. 'The witness who saw him said that Ben looked worried and perhaps even a little scared. I'm hoping that this was because the man he was talking to was his accomplice and Ben was looking worried because they were discussing their plans for the theft. Unfortunately, she couldn't tell us anything about the man as he had his back to her. However, there was a wedding reception taking place that same evening so I've asked Martin if he could have a look on social media. There's some nice facial recognition software he's used before and I'm hoping that one of the wedding guests might have included our man in the background of one of their photos on social media. I've given him the names of all the guests that attended the wedding so that might help him with the search.'

'A good idea,' Dan said. 'It would really help if we could narrow it down to just one of these. Hamish, do we have any idea of who the end customer might be?'

'Not yet but it would have to be someone with lots of money who also doesn't mind breaking the law. That painting's got blood on it and the customer will know that. He'd be someone quite powerful I'd guess.'

'What do you think would happen if this someone finds out that the painting is a fake?' Dan asked.

Hamish shrugged.

'I'd think it's quite possible that Mr. Linville wouldn't be breathing for long afterwards if that really is the case.'

'And our investigation would come to a dead end.' Dan said as he stood up. 'I'd better make a phone call. I need to make absolutely certain that Cathy Conyers keeps her little secret to herself for now.'

While Dan was on the phone Hamish asked, 'How are you doing Mac? I'd heard that you'd retired and yet here you are, still in the thick of things.'

'But not running the show though, thank God. Yes, I'm technically retired but I've made it clear to Dan and the team that if they need any help then they've only got to ask. Fortunately, they've been good enough to do just that. It's quite nice really, I just hand out some advice and the odd idea and then leave it up to Dan to make the decisions. We're lucky as he's quite good at that anyway.'

Hamish smiled, 'I must admit that I'm not surprised though. Personally, I could never see you being happy just pottering around the garden or whatever.'

Adil walked into the incident room and Mac noticed him do a double take when he saw Hamish. He came over.

'You're Hamish Hamilton!' Adil said excitedly.

'Yes, I guess I am.'

'I was there that day at Murrayfield. I saw that try you scored, the one that beat us. What a fantastic move that was! God, we were all cheering too and we were supporting the other side,' Adil said.

'Unfortunately, that was the last time we beat England but we've been getting better lately so who knows? I take it that you play yourself?' Hamish asked.

'Yes, for the British Police team. We're not bad but not in your league of course. That's amazing meeting you here of all places.' Adil said as he looked around. 'We're waiting for some chinless wonder of an art expert but it doesn't look like he's turned up yet.'

Mac coughed and nodded towards Hamish.

Adil looked mortified.

'No, you're not the art expert, are you? God, I'm so sorry, I was expecting...well, I don't know what I was expecting.'

Hamish roared with laughter.

'Don't worry, I get this all the time. I've even been mistaken for the art expert's minder at times.'

Dan returned.

'Thankfully, Miss Conyers is more than happy to keep it to herself. In fact, I think that she sounded quite relieved.' He looked over at Adil. 'I take it that you've introduced yourself to Hamish here.'

'Oh yes. It's been really nice meeting you, Hamish,' Adil said with a big smile before he went back to work.

Dan sat down again and noticed Mac glancing over at Martin.

'So, do you have any ideas as to what we should do next if we do manage to identify the mystery man as being one of these?' Dan asked.

'Well, the one bit of leverage we've got is the fact that it's a copy,' Hamish said. 'If we make this public knowledge then our man's life might not be worth much. So, it might be an idea to make contact with our thief and convince him that he's just passed a fake. If we offer him protection then who knows what he might be able to tell us.'

'We need to know which of these it is first though,' Mac said as he looked down at the photographs strewn across the table. 'If we pass this information on to the wrong man then it could well end any investigation right there and then.'

They sat around and tried some small talk for the next ten minutes or so while they waited. Mac couldn't help sneaking a glance over at Martin now and again but, every time he looked, he had his shoulders hunched down and his fingers were flying across the keyboard. He was beginning to think that his idea might be a dud until he caught a glimpse of movement out of the corner of his eye. It was Martin's arm going up in the air. Mac smiled.

Martin went over to the printer and then walked towards them with a smile from ear to ear.

'I think you might like this,' he said placing another photo on the table.

They all bent over the photo. It showed a man in a tuxedo with his bow tie undone. He was clearly the worse for drink and was pulling faces at the camera but in the background a man was caught as he was leaving the men's toilets. Martin had reprocessed the image so it was crisp and sharp. There could be no doubt.

It was definitely Sean Bernard Linville!

Chapter Fifteen

They all looked at the photo and then looked at each other.

'So, what do we do now?' Dan asked.

'Well, Linville lives in Paris so it looks like we'll need to get the French police involved. Luckily, I know someone who has a friend there, a friend who should be really able to help us with this,' Hamish said as he looked over at Mac.

'Yes, I'll get on to him right now,' Mac said with a smile desperately hoping that Vincent hadn't changed his number recently.

While Mac was on the phone Hamish explained.

'Mac's calling Commissaire Vincent Meyer. He's with the Police Judiciaire in Paris. Mac must have worked with him quite a few times before as they seemed to know each other quite well.'

'How did you get to meet him?' Dan asked.

'I met him when I was working with Mac on a case a couple of years ago where a painting had been stolen from the National Gallery. Our suspect had made a run for it to France.'

'And how did the case end?' Dan asked.

'Well, Vincent and his men were very good and they caught up with the thief just as he was about to get out of the country with the painting. I hope this one ends a bit better though.'

'Why did he escape?'

'Sort of,' Hamish replied. 'He shot himself once he knew he couldn't get away which was a pity. It would have been nice to know who'd commissioned the theft in the first place. There's a strong belief in some European police forces that many of these art thefts have been carried out by the same organisation. Now that would be the real prize, not just catching Linville but whoever put him up to it. We need to ensure that, whatever happens, we keep Sean Bernard Linville alive.'

Luckily Vincent hadn't changed his number. Mac gave the phone to Dan who told Vincent what they'd discovered so far. He was interested enough in the brief outline of the case he'd heard to set up an immediate conference call.

'Okay then Andy, Mac and Hamish we'll take the call,' Dan said. Then, turning to the team, he said in louder voice, 'I don't suppose anyone here speaks French, do they?'

The team all looked at each other and shook their heads. At the back of the room a hand went tentatively up.

'Is that you, Kate?' Dan asked.

She stood up and nodded.

'Do you really speak French?'

'Yes, I lived in Paris for most of my gap year when I was at university,' she explained.

'Well, you'd better join us then,' Dan said with a smile as he gestured towards the larger of the two interview rooms.

As they settled themselves down and waited for the call Mac said, 'By the way Vincent speaks excellent English.'

'That's this Commissaire Meyer?' Dan asked.

'Yes, we've worked together on at least ten or twelve cases over the years besides meeting up at various events and ceremonies,' Mac explained. 'My French is rubbish so the fact that his English was so good helped tremendously.'

The little room was quite crowded and Hamish taking up the place of two people didn't help much. Kate stood against the wall feeling out of place and almost wishing that she hadn't put her hand up. Dan stood up and offered Kate his seat.

'If we need you the microphone won't pick you up from way over there,' he explained.

She could see the logic of his argument and took his seat with good grace.

The phone rang and Dan put it on the speaker.

'Mac? Mac are you there?' a man's voice asked.

'Hello Vincent, yes I'm here. How are you?'

'I'm fine and Sylvie is too. So, straight to business. I'm sitting here with Thierry Rodrigues from the SDLCODF. I won't say the full name as it's quite a mouthful but his section deals with organised and financial crime and so he's interested in M. Linville on both counts.'

Dan introduced Andy and Hamish and then made a point of introducing Kate too. She raised her eyebrows as he did.

'So, Thierry and myself are both really hoping that you've got something for us,' Vincent said.

Dan explained the case as succinctly as he could. There was a silence at the other end that lasted for nearly a minute.

Eventually Vincent said, 'Well, you'd have to be here to see how excited my colleague Thierry is. He's punched the air once or twice so I think that you might be on to something.'

'Have you any idea who the end customer might be for the painting?' Hamish asked.

A new voice answered. His accent was heavier than Vincent's and he had to search for the correct word every now and then.

'Hello, I am Thierry Rodrigues. We're not sure who the end customer is but we think that the...er...person who commissioned the theft is a financier called Matthieu Cardini,' Thierry explained. 'He seems totally legitimate on the surface but we suspect that he's been involved in many crimes over the years including gun running, human trafficking, drugs, assassination and a lot more. He's originally from Corsica and he's rumoured to have strong links with the Union Corse and also with the Marseille criminal fraternity. We think that he's also been behind many of the recent art thefts. It's probably no coincidence that he's also a very big fan of Munch. He already owns four of his paintings but I'll leave you to guess which one, it's alleged, he's really after. So, it may well be that the end customer in this case is Cardini himself. If it is him then it's just as well that you managed to stop the news about it being a copy getting out. Cardini would not have taken the news well. He really doesn't like being crossed,' Thierry said.

'So, does this mean that if the news got out then Linville's life might be in danger?' Hamish asked.

'Very much so,' Thierry answered.

'In that case do you think that we might use this information to force Linville to turn himself in?' Hamish continued.

There was a moment of silence.

'Yes, it's possible,' Thierry eventually answered. 'If we can convince Linville that the painting is a copy then he might think it a better choice to give himself up to us rather than face whatever punishment Cardini might have planned for him.'

'So, where do we go from here then?' Dan asked.

'Well, we'd be grateful if you could let us have every-thing you've got in relation to the theft and murder,' Vincent replied. 'We've checked and it appears that M. Linville is currently in residence at his flat in Paris. As he's in our jurisdiction it becomes our case but I think it would help us both if you could send someone over to act as a liaison between our two forces. Of course, that someone must obviously have a good knowledge of the case and it would also help if they've had some previous experience of working with the Police Judiciaire. Do you have anyone like that in your team, do you think?'

All eyes turned towards Mac. Dan had to stop himself from laughing in order to assure Vincent that indeed they had. Dan looked over at Mac with a question on his face. Mac nodded.

'So, I think that's a yes. We'll try and get Mac to you as soon as possible,' Dan said. 'In the meantime, I'll send over everything we have and we'll start thinking about how we can best convince Linville that he has indeed just got a copy.'

At the end of the phone conversation Dan asked Kate to stay behind. Mac smiled as he had a good idea why. He started sorting out the travelling arrangements with Martin while he waited for her to come out.

'So, fancy having a travelling partner?' Kate asked.

Mac thought that she looking quite pleased with the prospect.

'I sure do and especially one who can speak the language. We're going by train and I'll pick up the tickets at Letchworth station. So, right now, I'm going straight home to pack a small case. What about you?' Mac asked.

'Could you drop me at the police station? My passport's in Dan's desk drawer. He had to copy it for some reason. I can get the train home and it'll only take me a few minutes to pack. If you give me a ring, I can jump on the same train that you're taking into London at Hatfield.'

'Sure. Come on then.'

As they drove Kate chatted away. It was the lightest he'd seen her since they met. He guessed that she really had a soft spot for Paris.

He packed a bag, checking twice that he had all his medication with him, and he was waiting at the train station less than an hour later. He rang Kate and told her that the train was just coming in and that he should be with her in about half an hour or so. She said that she was already on her way to the train station.

As it was only just after midday the train wasn't full and so Mac had been able to keep the seat beside him free for Kate. She gave him a quick smile but Mac thought that she looked quite strange and definitely different to when he'd seen her just over an hour or so before. The lightness had gone. She didn't say much on the way into London. She seemed to be thinking something through so Mac let her do so in peace.

In truth Kate's mind was in a whirl. Something had happened but she kept telling herself that it was nothing really. Except she knew that was a lie.

She'd gone to the police station to get her passport from Dan's desk and so she had to go through the double doors into the long corridor that led towards the team's room. A woman was walking down the corridor towards her. She was slim, taller than Kate and she wore a black trouser suit. Her hair was pulled back into a severe bun and she strode down the corridor with purpose. She had an open file in her hands that she was reading from as she walked. She didn't look up as she came towards her so Kate was able to look straight at her. She reckoned that the woman was a little older than her, mid-thirties perhaps. She had hardly any make up on but Kate thought that she was still very good looking.

These thoughts were just idle, flitting thoughts that came and went, until the second they passed each other that is.

Kate found the experience hard to describe in words. As she and woman passed each other she caught the smell of her perfume mingled with the natural smell of her body. It went straight to her head.

Kate suddenly felt intoxicated and a little wobbly on her feet. She had to stop walking and lean against the wall for a moment. She turned just in time to see the woman opening one of the double doors. She stopped, turned and looked back. She gave Kate a strange look but what did the look say? Kate wasn't sure. Then she was gone and that was it. It was nothing and it was over she told herself.

Except that she knew it wasn't.

Something had happened, something strange, something important even. She just wished that she had a clue what it was.

Chapter Sixteen

They were in a tunnel somewhere underneath the English Channel and Mac was staring out of the train window. It was dark outside and he was mostly looking at his own reflection. Kate was still quiet. However, she looked as if she'd calmed down a little so Mac tried some conversation.

'So, what was your little chat with Dan about?' Mac turned and asked. 'I'd guess that you've been officially appointed as my minder. Am I right?'

'You are,' Kate replied. 'Dan just wanted me to make sure that you didn't try and do too much. He said that he needs you to be at your best for as long as the case lasts. If you ask me though, I think he worries about you,' Kate replied. 'So, tell me, why did you pick the train?'

'I've heard that it's actually faster than flying to Paris if you factor in all the hanging about and transfers to and from the airport. But it wasn't that, if I'm honest I just hate flying these days.'

'Why is that? You don't strike me as being the scared type,' Kate asked.

'I don't mind the flying, so long as the flight's not too long that is. No, it's all the kerfuffle in getting to and from the plane itself that I can't stand. I can't walk far these days and it seems like every departure gate is a mile and a half away from the departure lounge. That means that I need help and the standard of help in UK airports for disabled people is variable to say the least. I flew over to Ireland a while back. In Ireland it was great, no hanging around and I had a bit of a craic with the people who were helping me. When I got back here though I had to wait over an hour on the plane before someone was available to wheel me away. I felt a right idiot as there was just me that needed help and the whole of the cabin crew and both pilots had to hang around until I got off. Never again if I can help it,' Mac said with feeling. 'No, the train's better. I can even get up and walk around for a while if my back gets too stiff.'

'I never thought about it like that.' She could hear the annoyance in Mac's voice so she thought it would be as well to change the subject. 'So, tell me. How did you get to know this Commissaire Meyer?'

'It was a long time ago now,' Mac said with a smile. 'The first time we met, I was just a Detective Sergeant accompanying my old boss DCS Rob Graveley to Paris on a case. I'd never been there before and I remember that I couldn't get rid of the notion that I'd somehow walked onto a massive movie set. The city looked so beautiful and strange, yet I had this tremendous feeling of déjà vu, probably because of all the films I'd seen that were set in Paris, I suppose. Anyway, Vincent was a Brigadier at the time and he was accompanying his boss too. I've never been quite sure about the police ranks in France but it seemed that we were at about the same level, although Brigadier sounds a lot grander than Sergeant, I must admit. Luckily, we found time to have a few drinks together and we really got on well. Over the years we got to know each other even better as there were always investigations that needed some cross-border cooperation. Vincent and his wife Sylvie even came and stayed with us a few times when they were visiting London.'

'When was the last time you saw him?'

'Oh, about nine months before...before I left the force. He was over on some sort of ceremonial visit and popped in to see me at the station.'

He'd almost said 'before Nora died'. Vincent had sent a card and flowers and had phoned on quite a few occasions. He'd even offered to come and see him but Mac had put him off just as he had everyone else.

146

'So, I'd guess that you know Paris a lot better than I do if you lived here for a year. How did that happen?' Mac asked.

'I had a university gap year and I decided to spend the time studying the French judicial system. It's based on the Napoleonic Code while ours is based on Common Law so it's quite different. I studied at the Sorbonne and it was a good time for me. I lived in a single room near the Left Bank and there was always a party going on somewhere.'

'Even so, studying in a gap year? I always thought that they were for fun, for travelling and for finding yourself, whatever that is.'

Kate smiled.

'I'm afraid that I was a bit of a law nerd in those days and I actually enjoyed it. If I'm being honest being away from home helped a lot too,' she said as the smile disappeared.

Mac felt that she'd touched on at least one source of her unhappiness. He didn't say anything and waited to see if she wanted to speak about it.

'But that's another story,' she said. 'Anyway, there is a question I wanted to ask, if you don't mind that is?'

She was obviously changing the subject which was okay with Mac.

'Now that depends on the question,' he replied.

'I was surprised when I found out that your real name is Dennis. So how did you end up being called Mac?'

'Everyone who knew me before I went into the police calls me Denny. I unfortunately got the name on my first day in the force,' Mac said with a frown.

'Why unfortunately?' Kate asked. 'Mac's not that bad as nicknames go.'

'I suppose it isn't but mine has a little baggage.'

Mac paused for a moment. Very few people knew the story behind his nickname and for good reason. He wondered momentarily if he should tell Kate the whole

147

story and he eventually decided that he should. If he could make a confession to her then, perhaps, she might find it easier to tell him about what was so obviously bothering her.

'Okay, it was my first day in uniform. I was nineteen, wet behind the ears and more than a little frightened at finding myself in the hustle and bustle of a very big police station. I had to report to one of the sergeants who was about to become the ruler of my life while I was stationed there. This was back in the eighties and things were a lot different then. I hear people in the force moan about change nowadays but, as far as I'm concerned, most of the changes in the police since then have been good ones. Back then it was basically okay to be racist and misogynist and just about compulsory to be anti-gay.

Anyway, I turned up at this sergeant's desk to report for work and part of his job, as he saw it, was to hand out the nicknames for the new recruits. For some reason everyone in those days had to have a nickname, although God knows why. For instance, just before me there was someone called Jones and this sergeant gave him the nickname Taffy even though he said that he'd never been to Wales and his family had lived in the Midlands for hundreds of years. So, I was a bit nervous when he asked me my name. I told him but he obviously misheard me and took my name to be 'MacGuire' rather than 'Maguire'. In his somewhat limited mind, any name that began with the prefix 'Mac' just had to come from Scotland and so my nickname became 'Mac'. He used to take the piss by putting on a fake Scottish accent and saying 'Och aye the noo!' and then asking me if I was keeping my bagpipes in good condition.'

'Well, that doesn't sound so bad,' Kate said.

'The only problem was I went along with it. My name, Maguire, is Irish, my parents were Irish and I was born in Ireland. I suppose at the time it just seemed...well, easier to just say nothing.'

Kate was thoughtful for a moment.

'Yes, that wasn't long after the Birmingham pub bombings was it?'

'No, not too long. I knew people who were injured in the bombings too, friends. Anyway, you could say that being Irish wasn't exactly popular with many people at the time and even more so in the force. So, for a while at least, I sort of denied my background by saying nothing and it's never sat right with me since. I mean to everyone outside of my family it's my name now, whether I like it or not, but I'm not altogether proud of it.'

'Yes, I can see that but you were so young at the time,' Kate said. 'You surely don't blame yourself, do you?'

'No, not totally anyway,' Mac replied. 'But it feels so unjust that a mistake you make when you're so young and clueless can follow you around for the rest of your life,' Mac said. 'Anyway, it's certainly made me feel a lot more sympathetic to other people who've made mistakes too, even when it's of the criminal kind.'

'Yes, we all make mistakes, I suppose, but the real trick is in knowing that it was a mistake and doing your best to make things right or, at least, to not repeat it. Some people just don't have that capacity, to them everything they do is right and everyone else is wrong. I suppose that Tommy told you all about my father?' Kate asked.

'No, Tommy never mentioned him.'

Kate had told Tommy about her father when they'd been working together on the Whyte case. She suddenly felt a little ashamed for thinking that he would have told anyone else what had been discussed in a private conversation.

'Let's not mention him then,' Kate said. 'It might just spoil a nice trip. There is something else I wanted to ask you though. When I was at the station picking up my passport, I saw a woman there. She was quite tall and had a black trouser suit on.'

'Did she have her hair pulled back into a bun?' Mac asked.

'Yes, that's right. I take it that you know her then? It's just that I hadn't seen her before and I was just wondering who she was, that's all.'

Mac could see that Kate was trying to make it sound like she was just asking this to pass the time but he couldn't help noticing a slight reddening of her pale cheeks and her breath speeding up a little. This was getting interesting.

'Yes, I've worked with her on a couple of cases now. She used to be Andy Reid's sergeant when he ran the local detective team at Letchworth. When he left to join our team, she got promoted to Detective Inspector and she's running the team now.'

'Oh, she's a DI.' There was a longish pause before Kate asked, 'What's her name?'

Mac was fairly certain now that her question hadn't been an idle one.

'It's Toni, Toni Woodgate,' he replied.

'Tony?'

'Yes, but with an 'I'. It's short for Antonia I think.'

Her mouth silently made the shape of the word.

'She's a really good copper,' Mac said. 'I was glad that they had the sense to promote her. She'll do a good job for them.'

Kate was silent for a while. Then she shook her head as if to clear it and gave Mac a somewhat embarrassed smile.

They still had the better part of an hour to go when Kate changed the subject once again. She started talking about her time in Paris and, as interesting as Mac found it, he still found himself thinking about what she'd said and probably more about what she didn't say. Before long the train came to a stop and they were in Paris.

The Gare du Nord was a railway station so grand that Mac always thought that it put most cathedrals to shame.

As he walked away from the train and looked around, he thought that the huge space might indeed be big enough to house at least two or three fair sized cathedrals. On Vincent's instructions they caught a taxi straight to their hotel. It took quite a while before they reached their destination as the driver had to dodge in and out of the traffic and they got stuck in traffic jams more than once. Mac looked out at the wide boulevards, the beautiful stone-faced buildings, the people sitting outside the cafes, talking, reading, even kissing and he felt some-thing of the outright awe he'd felt on his very first visit. Then they were suddenly no longer hemmed in by buildings and the space gloriously opened up around them as they crossed over the river at the Pont Neuf.

The bridge itself was lined with ornate street lamps that reminded him of the old gas lamps that used to light the streets when he'd been a child. However, it was the view down the length of the Seine that held his eye. It was stunning. The water sparkled in the early evening sunlight and his eye was drawn towards the series of bridges that ran across the wide river further down. A massive tourist boat glided lazily away from them leaving a long wake glittering behind it. Both sides of the river were lined with grand buildings some five or six storeys high. Their ornate facades were decorated with warm honey-coloured stone and long windows. Some had conical turrets that looked as if they belonged to some fairy tale castle.

Once over the river Mac knew that they were now in the Left Bank. Here they drove down some very narrow streets lined with little shops and cafes until they turned into a river of cars on the wide and busy Boulevard Saint-Germain. The taxi turned into a side street and stopped.

The hotel had been recommended by Vincent as it wasn't too far away from the Quai des Orfevres where the headquarters of the Police Judiciaire were situated and where Vincent worked. It was only a three-star hotel but it was more than luxurious enough for Mac. The room was small but very comfortable and, best of all, it had a quite lovely view over the rooftops of Paris.

He looked out and wished that Nora could have been there with him too, he knew that she'd have loved it. He was shaken out of his reverie by his phone going off. It was a text from Vincent. He said that he'd meet them in the hotel bar in forty-five minutes or so. He rang Kate and asked her to meet him downstairs in the bar when she was ready.

He quickly washed, shaved and changed his shirt. When he was finished, he looked at himself in the full-length mirror and sighed. It brought back the memory of a family event he'd attended when he'd been a child.

A sharp-tongued aunt of his had looked at another woman and said, 'She thinks she's gorgeous but she looks no better than a bag of spuds in that dress.'

Mac hadn't known what she'd meant at the time but he did now. He tore himself away from the mirror and took the lift downstairs.

Kate was waiting for him. She'd put some make-up on and had changed from her usual business-like trouser suit into a light and flowing russet coloured strapless dress that went very well with her flame red hair.

'Well, you look different!' Mac said with some surprise.

In fact, he thought that she looked quite stunning.

'Well, I thought that, as I was in Paris, then I might as well dress for the occasion. Do you want a drink?'

'Yes please. A beer would be great.'

She got the waiter's attention and said something very quickly in French. Mac caught the word 'biere' but very little else.

'What was that you ordered for yourself?' he asked.

'Kir with crème de châtaigne.'

'What on earth is that?'

'It's an aperitif, basically white wine with chestnut liqueur,' Kate said. 'I used to drink it a lot when I lived here.'

The drinks arrived and, while his beer was crisp and refreshing, he thought that Kate's drink looked very interesting indeed. He decided that he'd let Kate make the decisions when it came to food and drinks as she obviously knew what she was doing. He remembered back to the first time he'd visited a Parisian restaurant by himself. He'd ordered 'steak haché' because it had sounded interesting. He thought that he was ordering something exotic but he'd ended up with a hamburger. It was a very good hamburger but he'd been more than a little disappointed.

Mac stood up when he saw Vincent come through the door. He came towards Mac with arms open wide and gave him a hug and then kissed him on both cheeks. Mac remembered Vincent's wife Sylvie mischievously pointing out to Nora that Mac got more kisses than she did sometimes.

'Hello, old friend. How are you?' Vincent asked.

Mac looked at his friend and colleague. He hadn't changed much apart from the fact that his jet-black hair was now going grey at the sides. Vincent was a handsome man and looked more like a Gallic film star than anything else. He remembered the few times that he'd visited Mac at the police station in London and how most of his female colleagues had looked twice when he walked into the room. Now he thought of it, one or two of his male colleagues had done exactly the same too. Yet, Mac had also noticed that Vincent was apparently unaware of his attractiveness and thankfully any narcissistic tendencies had just passed him by.

He thought that his friend had aged much better than he had. Vincent looked distinguished while Mac just looked like a bag of spuds.

153

'I'm better now Vincent, better that I was anyway. And you?'

'I'm fine and so is Sylvie. She sends you her best.'

Only then did Vincent glance over at Kate.

'And who's this?' he asked with a big smile as he gave Kate an appraising look.

Mac could see that he was impressed. She seemed quite impressed too judging by the smile on her face.

'This is Detective Sergeant Kate Grimsson,' Mac said.

'A sergeant?' Vincent said in wonder as he shook her hand.

Kate said something in French and Vincent replied. He then turned back to Mac.

'Ah, we were born too early my friend. You know when I was young it took me some time to make the decision to join the police but, if we'd have had sergeants like Kate back in those days, I don't think I'd have thought twice. Now it's my turn to introduce you to someone,' Vincent said.

A man who had been standing quietly behind Vincent came forward and shook Mac's hand and then Kate's. He was younger than Vincent and quite ordinary looking. He was balding and had a self-effacing air about him. Mac couldn't help feeling an immediate affinity with him.

'Let me introduce my friend and colleague, Thierry Rodrigues, who you spoke to on the phone,' Vincent said.

They sat down and Vincent ordered a round of drinks.

'Well, your news certainly gave us some hope of nailing Cardini but we have to be careful and 'fly under the radar' as you say and that's why we arranged to meet you here first rather than at the Quai,' Vincent explained. 'Unfortunately, we feel it's quite possible that M. Cardini's tentacles might have spread into the police as well.'

'So, what now?' Mac asked.

'Well, we know that Linville is in Paris and is spreading money around,' Thierry said. 'If we can contact him and convince him that the painting is indeed a fake then we might have a chance. Linville would have nowhere to go except to us.'

'The only problem is in convincing him that the copy he's passed on to Cardini really is a fake,' Vincent said. 'He's bound to think that it's some sort of trick.'

'Our art expert Hamish Hamilton is working on that at the moment,' Mac replied. 'He said that he had an idea but he wouldn't tell us what it was until he made some calls. We'll hopefully know something by tomorrow.'

'In the meantime, we've got a team who are keeping an eye on Linville twenty-four hours a day,' Vincent said. 'I don't want to take any chances as he has the bad habit of often being in two places at once.'

'What do you mean by 'two places at once'?' Mac asked remembering that Hamish had said something about Linville always having an alibi.

'Well, the German police thought they had him once, as did the Spanish police just last year,' Thierry explained. 'They'd built up a beautiful case with lots of circumstantial evidence and even some biometric measurements from some CCTV footage, you know height, arm length and so on. However, every time someone gets close, he comes up with a cast-iron alibi. So, while all this evidence identified him as being the thief who stole a Rothko from the Museo Nacional in Madrid, he was also seen that same night over a thousand kilometres away dining at one of Paris's finest restaurants. So, it was some circumstantial evidence against the testimony of twenty or more people and some verified time-stamped CCTV footage. This was also backed up with more CCTV footage taken at his apartment block. So, all that work by the Spanish police was basically for nothing.'

'I see what you mean,' Mac replied, 'and yet you still seem to think it was him?'

'We have our own sources of information, as I'm sure that you do, and they all point the finger at Linville. Yet we never seem to be able to get any hard evidence to back it up,' Thierry said looking somewhat exasperated.

'Well, maybe this is the time that we get Linville at last. We can only wait and see what Hamish comes up with,' Vincent said. 'So, now for the most important question of all. Have you eaten yet?'

Vincent took them to a little restaurant just around the corner where he said that they did the best Moules-Frites in Paris. He was right. The mussels, cooked in white wine and garlic, had a real flavour of the sea while the frites were golden and crunchy. It was a really nice combination.

It was good to catch up with his old friend and to hear what he and his wife Sylvie had been up to since they'd last met. Vincent said that she'd asked if she could meet up with Mac before he left Paris. At some point in the evening Vincent and Kate got talking about her time in Paris. He could see that some mild flirting was going on but Mac knew that Kate was as safe as houses with Vincent. He was definitely a one-woman man and that woman was Sylvie.

He started chatting to Thierry Rodrigues who hadn't said much so far.

'Vincent's told me about you,' Thierry said. 'I'm sorry for your loss.'

'Thanks,' Mac said.

He suddenly couldn't think of anything else to say.

'I believe that you've now retired and that you've become a private detective?'

'Yes, that's right,' Mac replied. 'I've got some back problems unfortunately.'

'Yes, I know. You've heard of the Maigret books?' Thierry asked.

'Oh yes, I've read just about all of them I'd guess, over the years that is.'

'Well, Simenon based the character of Jules Maigret on a real police detective called Chief Inspector Marcel Guillaume who worked here in Paris before the war. He retired from the police at the age of fifty-five, something that he apparently wasn't too happy about. However, he had no choice in the matter as that was the compulsory retirement age in those days. He never stopped working though. He too became a private detective after he left the police and he carried on working successfully as a detective for some decades afterwards, I believe.'

'Really?' Mac said in some surprise.

'Yes really. When Vincent told me about you it brought it to mind. So, here's a toast to many more decades as a detective,' Thierry said as he raised his glass.

They clinked glasses and, hearing the sound, Vincent turned around and demanded to know what they were drinking to. Thierry told them what he'd just said to Mac and they repeated the toast again with everyone clinking glasses this time.

The party broke up shortly after this as Vincent had to go back to headquarters to check on something. Mac was quite relieved as he was starting to feel tired.

Kate was on the same floor as him but further down the hallway so she stopped outside his room to say goodnight.

'Did you have a good time?' Mac said as he opened his door.

'Yes, I did. Your friend Vincent is a very nice man,' she replied with a smile. 'Oh, and Thierry's very nice too,' she hastily added.

Mac smiled. His friend hadn't lost his touch then.

'Good night then, Kate,' he said. 'Hopefully tomorrow's going to be a busy day.'

'Good night, Mac,' she said as she walked down the hall towards her room.

Mac thought about what Thierry had said as he lay in the unfamiliar, but not uncomfortable, bed while he

157

waited for sleep to come. He thought that Thierry was quite a kind and thoughtful type of person and, if his intention had been to inspire him with his tale of Marcel Guillaume, Mac decided that he'd succeeded.

A short while after this sleep overtook him and he slept deeply throughout the night.

Chapter Seventeen

The wonderful aromas of fresh coffee and warm pastry hit Mac as soon as he walked out of the lift. All he had to do was follow his nose to find the breakfast room. Kate was already there. She was back in her black trouser suit and she was drinking from an outsize cup of milky coffee. Mac sat down opposite her. On the other side of the window the gigantic movie set called Paris was already teeming with life.

'Have you eaten yet?' Mac asked.

'No, I've just had coffee. I thought that I'd wait until you turned up. I'm hoping that it's going to be an exciting day today,' Kate said with an expectant smile.

'Yes, me too but it will only be exciting if Hamish can come up with something. I suppose that we'll just have to wait and see what it is.'

He wished that Hamish hadn't been so secretive. He was itching to find out what he had up his sleeve.

Kate attracted the waitress's attention and ordered coffee for Mac and croissants for them both.

'It's strange sometimes how one case can lead to another, isn't it?' Kate said. 'I mean originally we'd have been happy just to catch Ben Meeks' murderer but now the target is this Cardini who's some sort of super-criminal from what Thierry said.'

'It's even stranger than that,' Mac said. 'For me it all started off with a missing dog and now here I am in Paris on a major international case.'

For some reason thinking of dogs suddenly brought to mind his other case, the alleged murder of Albert Ginn by Father Pat Curran. There was something there, the ghost of an idea perhaps, but he couldn't quite put his finger on it. He mentally filed it away until later.

Mac's phone rang. It was Dan.

'Hello Mac. I've got a very excited Hamish here who wants to have a word,' Dan said as he handed the phone over.

'Mac, I think I might just have cracked it. I'm sorry I couldn't tell you what I had in mind before you left. I had to make sure that a particular person would be willing to help first because without him my idea wouldn't have got off the ground. I've contacted Professor Morten Halvorsen from the Munch Museum in Oslo and, luckily, he's willing to cooperate. I didn't know it but apparently he's been dying to see Miss Conyers' painting for some time.'

'So, how exactly can he help?' Mac asked.

'Well, he's just about the most trusted expert in the world when it comes to Munch. If he could examine the painting and confirm that it's genuine and do it on video too then that might just convince Linville.'

'And Linville would believe this Professor Halvorsen?'

'If Linville knows his art as well as I think he does then he'll believe him alright,' Hamish said. 'Professor Halvorsen is well known for his integrity and for the fact that he sees himself as safeguarding Munch's legacy for future generations. He was once offered ten million euros in cash to confirm that a fake Munch was real.'

'What happened?' Mac asked.

'He went straight to the police and they put a wire on him when the offer was made. It was real too, the offer I mean, ten million euros in five hundred euro notes were found in a suitcase. Believe me, Professor Halvorsen will only say the painting's genuine if it really is genuine and Linville will know that,' Hamish said.

'That's great! It looks like we have a plan then,' Mac said with some relief.

'With some luck we should be able to get the video to you around mid-day. The professor's caught an early flight and it's only a couple of hours flying time from Oslo. All the arrangements have been made and I'll be

160

picking him up myself at the airport and taking him straight to the bank. I'll ring you once the professor's finished,' Hamish explained. 'Here, I'll pass you back to Dan.'

Mac waited while the phone changed hands.

'That sounds like it might work,' Dan said.

'It certainly does but what happens after the professor validates the painting?' Mac asked.

'We'll need to figure out a secure way of getting the video to you in Paris and then it will be up to you and the French police to work out how to quietly get the video to Linville,' Dan said.

'Okay then, I'll contact Vincent and tell him the good news,' Mac said.

Vincent was delighted with Hamish's plan and said that he'd send someone over to pick up Mac and Kate straight away. They waited on the corner of the boulevard which was no hardship. The day was bright and sunny and the pavement cafes were doing good business. It was nice just standing there in the sunshine for a moment and watching the comings and goings. A few minutes later a police car pulled up and Mac and Kate got in.

'Thierry, good morning,' Mac said with some surprise. 'I wasn't expecting you to be picking us up.'

'It was on my way in so I was glad to do it. Did you sleep well?' he asked as he drove off.

'Very well thanks. I take it that Vincent has told you about the plan?'

'Yes, that's why I'm joining him at the Quai. It sounds like your expert might have something there. Linville knows his art so I'd guess that he'll be well aware of who this Professor Halvorsen is.'

'I was just wondering about the problem of getting the video to Linville though and also how we might communicate with him after that. If Cardini's the man you say he is then he'll probably have someone keeping an eye on Linville just in case.'

Thierry smiled.

'Yes, I've just been thinking about that too and I believe that we have a plan. I'll tell you all about it when we get to the Quai.'

A few minutes later the car pulled up outside a huge and impressive four-storied grey stone building with columns all along the front and ornate decorations above each window. Mac remembered the first time that he'd visited this building. If someone had told him that it was a royal palace or even a museum he wouldn't have been surprised. However, this was the Paris headquarters of the Police Judiciaire and it was quite a lot grander than his old police station in London.

After what seemed like a half a mile of corridors and a lift to the third floor, they found Vincent and the team that he'd put together for the operation.

Vincent welcomed them and introduced them to everyone. There were eight people in the room including a young eager looking man who Vincent introduced as his assistant Christophe Clement. Christophe explained that most of the team were out keeping track of Linville. Mac could see that the team were all excited and he could well understand it. They'd been after Linville for years and they could all sense that they might be very close to taking the best art thief in Europe.

'So, I've been in contact with Hamish and he's going to send the video to me via a VPN network link that one of my technical people has just activated,' Vincent said. 'Hopefully that should be more than secure enough. Once we've got the video, we'll put it on a DVD. I'll let Thierry tell you what will happen next.'

'M. Linville is very careful. He doesn't own a computer or even a smart TV,' Thierry explained. 'He buys cheap pay phones when he needs them and destroys the old ones and he never uses email or any kind of social media. We know that he must keep in contact with potential clients somehow and we suspect that this must be done by some sort of physical means.'

'Like the spies in the fifties then, using dead drops, passing newspapers and the like?' Mac asked.

'Yes and, if that is the case, he's good at it too as we haven't figured out how he does it yet,' Thierry said. 'He's a player, he likes playing games and he seems to like playing with us most of all.'

'And he also has the happy knack of appearing to be in two places at the same time,' Mac added.

'Yes, I only wish that we knew how he did that. Anyway, with regard to getting the video to Linville I think that we've had a stroke of luck. Our men have been shadowing him and one of them has discovered that Linville's ordered a book from a specialist bookshop. He's supposed to be picking it up at around three o'clock this afternoon. If we can get the video in time then I think we might be able to pass it to him in the book.'

'How can you be sure that he'll definitely pick it up today though?' Mac asked.

'Because that's what he's said to the bookshop's owner,' Thierry replied. 'Anyway, we know that he won't hang around. He's been waiting for this book to arrive for some time.'

'What is it, the book?' Kate asked.

'Linville is a bit of a cinéphile…' Thierry paused and looked at Vincent for the word in English.

'A film buff,' Kate suggested.

Thierry smiled gratefully at Kate and continued, 'Yes that's it, a film buff. The book is a scholarly work about his favourite director.'

'Who's that?' Mac asked expecting the answer to be some obscure French auteur.

'Clint Eastwood. Linville is crazy about his films. My idea is to put the video on a DVD and attach it to the inside of the book as though it's a part of it.'

'But how will he know that it's come from us?' Kate asked.

'We'll put a label on the DVD that says 'To the True Mr. Wales'. He said that to me once in an interview. He'll know who it's from,' Thierry said.

Mac had to think for a minute.

'Oh, that's right. One of Eastwood's films was called 'The Outlaw Josey Wales', wasn't it?'

'Yes, and Linville thinks that he's the modern version of the Western outlaw. That's all very romantic until you remember that he's just a thief and a murderer too. Anyway, we know that he's got every Eastwood film ever made and he uses a DVD player to play them. Hopefully he'll be intrigued enough to play the DVD as soon as he gets the book and, once he does, then he'll realise that his choices will be getting very limited indeed.'

'That's very clever.' Mac was impressed. 'It looks like you've thought of everything. How will you make it easy for Linville to give himself up though if that's what he decides to do?'

'We'll be waiting in a van outside,' Thierry said. 'It will have a sign on it saying 'Lafayette Espadrilles'. I'm sure he'll get it.'

'Espadrilles? They're shoes, aren't they?' Mac asked with a puzzled expression.

'It's a play on words,' Thierry replied. 'One of Clint Eastwood's earliest films, in which he only had a small part, was called the 'Lafayette Escadrille' which means Lafayette Squadron. I haven't seen it but it's supposed to be about American pilots who fought for France in the First World War. We're fairly certain that Linville will immediately guess that the van belongs to us.'

'It sounds as if you've thought of everything,' Mac said.

'Perhaps but now all we can do is wait for the video to come through,' Vincent said. 'I have to admit that I've had a thought and it's one I don't like. What if the Professor finds that it's the one in the bank vault that's the fake?'

They all looked at each other and no-one could think of anything to say. Mac thought that this was unlikely yet, now that Vincent had mentioned it as a possibility, he couldn't get it out of his head. The seconds ticked away while they waited for Hamish to contact them. Kate went out of the room and came back with two coffees one of which Mac gratefully accepted.

Mac took his phone out and checked just in case but there were no messages. The whole room went quiet and everyone was just waiting. When Mac's phone rang to tell him that he had a text message he almost jumped. He pulled his phone out and read it.

'Prof has confirmed genuine. Video on its way to you. H'

Mac let out a sigh of relief. It was only when he looked up that he noticed that everyone in the room was looking at him. He smiled and gave the thumbs up and he could feel the tension leave the room. A few seconds later Christophe smiled and said something to Vincent.

'They've got the video,' Kate said to Mac.

'We've received the video and we should have the DVD ready in the next few minutes,' Vincent confirmed a few minutes later. 'We'll pass it on to one of our men who've been regularly using the bookshop and he'll insert it into the book. Once Linville's picked it up, we'll follow him. My guess is that he'll most likely head back to his flat once he has the book and after that we can only hope.'

Thierry said his goodbyes. As he was someone that Linville knew, he was going to join the team in the van and hopefully welcome Linville inside.

Mac looked at the clock on the wall, it was now twelve forty. He settled down to wait. He glanced over at Kate who was following all the conversations that were going on between the team. Mac was so glad that she was here. He couldn't understand a word that they were saying and she'd make sure that he knew what the team knew.

At five minutes past one Vincent came over and confirmed that the DVD had been successfully inserted into the book.

'Is the owner of the bookshop in on it?' Mac asked.

Vincent shook his head.

'Our man told the owner that he was really interested in buying a copy of the book too so he arranged to have a quick look at it before Linville was due to pick it up. It's a very expensive book so we reckoned that the owner wouldn't turn down a prospective sale. We would have involved the owner if we had to but the less people who know about this the better.'

Again, Mac was impressed. He noticed Vincent had started drumming his fingers on the table.

'I'm never good at times like this,' Vincent explained. 'I always feel a bit like a football manager. You've decided on your tactics and picked your players but, once the whistle blows, it's mostly up to them. All you can do is watch from the side lines and worry.'

'I know exactly how you feel. So, what happens now?' Mac asked.

'We've got several men staking out the bookshop. We should have a live feed from there before long. At around two thirty we'll get the van in position and we'll have another live feed from outside the flat as well so we can see what happens if Linville does decide to turn himself in.'

'So, we'll see it all on live TV?' Kate asked in some surprise.

'Well, some of it anyway. So, now on to my main job for the moment. What sandwiches would you like?' Vincent asked with a smile.

Mac was surprised to find that he was hungry again and he noticed that Kate must also have felt quite peckish as she ordered one as well. Mac had a sudden craving for a police canteen sausage and egg sandwich but he settled for a ham, brie and tomato baguette instead.

At two fifteen a couple of the team moved a very large TV on a stand into the centre of the room. They then turned it on and started fiddling about with the remote control. The screen burst into life and showed a narrow street on the other side of which a brasserie stood on the corner. Little tables stood on the pavement at which people were sitting and talking and drinking. Next to the brasserie there was a neat little shop with books in the window. 'The Serious Bookshop - Livres sur le cinéma' the sign said above the window.

'It's just like going to the cinema too, isn't it?' Mac said to Kate. 'I just hope that this feature's quite boring though; man buys book, man walks home, man comes out, man gets into van, van drives off. That'd do it for me.'

However, Mac was also aware that things rarely went exactly to plan so he could only keep hoping for the best.

As three o'clock approached more of the team stopped working and started staring at the TV screen. Just before three, a dark-haired man walked towards the bookshop.

'C'est lui, c'est Linville!' Christophe said out loud.

Kate told him that Linville had arrived but the team's excitement had already told Mac that it was him. Linville left a few minutes later with a very large book in a very large plastic bag. The camera tracked him until he disappeared around the corner.

Vincent joined them again.

'So, now we wait until he turns up at his flat. It's not far away so it shouldn't take him more than six or seven minutes to get there.'

It was eight minutes before he appeared in shot as he opened the front door of an expensive looking block of flats.

'So, now we wait and hope,' Vincent said.

The team waited and watched in almost total silence. A few people came and went from the apartment block but none of them were Linville. Mac looked at the clock and the second hand seemed to be moving in slow motion. Everything depended on what Linville would do next. Everyone's nerves were well frayed before Linville finally came out of the door just before four o'clock. He looked up and down the street and then stared straight at the camera. He nodded his head and gave the camera a little smile of resignation before he started across the street.

'He's giving himself up!' Vincent said. 'I never thought I'd see this...'

Vincent was interrupted by the sound of rapid gunfire. Linville collapsed in a heap in the middle of the road and a split second later the camera went black.

It too had been hit.

Chapter Eighteen

The team immediately went into action. Some rushed out of the room while others picked up their phones. The room was filled with a babble of voices competing to be heard. All Mac and Kate could do was sit and wait to find out exactly what had just happened. Kate gave Mac snippets of the conversations she could hear but it didn't make much sense to them as yet. It was a very long fifteen minutes before Vincent joined them again and gave them an update.

'Here's what we know so far. As Linville crossed the street a man behind him pulled a machine pistol out of a shopping bag and sprayed him with bullets. We reckon that Linville was hit at least eight times. He died more or less instantly. Some of the bullets also hit our van and one of them hit the camera destroying it.'

'Was anyone in the van hurt?' Mac asked thinking about Thierry.

'Luckily no, which is a small miracle considering. The assassin, after killing Linville, then threw a package onto his body and ran off. He was picked up a few metres down the road by a motorcycle and they sped off into traffic. We tried to follow but we lost them.'

'What was the package that the murderer threw?' Mac asked.

'Here,' Vincent said handing them a photograph.

It was a rectangular package wrapped in clear plastic. Inside Mac could see that it was a painting of a young naked woman. It had been slashed diagonally from corner to corner with a knife.

'Cathy Conyers' Munch,' Mac said. 'I take it that Cardini had discovered for himself that it was a fake. Do you think that they aimed for the van on purpose?'

'We can't be sure but we think that it just happened to be in the line of fire,' Vincent said.

'So, what now?' Kate asked.

Mac thought that this was a very good question. They both looked at Vincent.

He shrugged and said with a frown, 'Well, Linville's dead and, as we've got absolutely nothing on Cardini, I'd guess that's it.'

Mac gave this some thought.

'Would you mind if we went over to the crime scene?'

'No, not at all,' Vincent said with a despondent shrug. 'I'll get someone to drop you over.'

As Vincent walked away Mac could tell from his body language that his friend was absolutely gutted by what had just happened. He guessed that when those bullets hit Linville, the case died too.

Vincent told them that a police car would arrive in a few minutes to take them to the crime scene. By the time they made it onto the street outside a uniformed policeman was waiting for them in an unmarked car. He sped off through the busy streets, siren blaring, and Mac literally had to hang on to his seat. He asked Kate to tell the driver to slow down and kill the sirens. The person they were going to see wasn't going anywhere.

To Mac's relief the rest of the drive was somewhat quieter and far less bumpy. They pulled up just the other side of the crime scene tape that ran right across the street. The press were already there in force taking photographs from a distance while two journalists were talking to camera.

Mac saw Thierry standing on the pavement watching the activity with interest and waved to him. Thierry came over and held up the tape for them to come through. To his left Mac could see the police van. He counted the bullet holes in the side of the van. There were seven in all. In front of him a scrum of forensics people in white suits were crawling around on the floor.

Mac could see that Thierry looked quite shaken.

'You were lucky today,' he said.

'We were,' Thierry replied.

Kate noticed that drops of blood were falling from Thierry's right ear lobe. It looked as if a small piece had been taken out of it at the bottom.

'Thierry, your ear,' she said offering him a packet of paper handkerchiefs that she always carried with her when travelling.

Thierry dabbed at his ear and then looked at the blood colouring the paper. He went quite white for a few seconds and Mac couldn't blame him.

'One of the bullets, I heard it whizz by, but it was obviously closer than I'd thought. Looks like another couple of millimetres...' he said leaving the sentence hanging.

Mac and Kate gave each other a look. That really was too close for comfort.

Thierry shook his head to clear it.

'Do you want to see the body?' he asked.

Mac nodded. They walked forward a few steps and Mac at last met Sean Bernard Linville. He'd fallen on his front but the head was on one side so Mac could see his profile. The bullet wounds could be clearly seen on his back. Whoever killed him knew what they were doing. They'd made absolutely sure than Linville was dead. A few feet away he could see the painting being attended to by several members of the forensic team.

'Vincent was saying that he didn't think that they were aiming specifically at the van,' Mac said.

'I'd tend to agree,' Thierry said as they walked back onto the pavement. 'The murderer was obviously waiting for Linville to come out and, as soon as he appeared, he went behind him and shot him in the back. We think that he used a PP-2000. It's a Russian-made machine pistol, a very powerful weapon. He then threw the painting onto Linville's body and ran to the corner just there where a motorcycle was waiting for him. In the traffic he knew no-one would have a chance of following him. It was all very professionally done.'

'Yes, it looks that way, doesn't it?' Mac said. 'Would you mind if we had a look at his flat?'

'Sure, follow me.'

Thierry led them into a lift and took them up to the top floor.

'Do you mind if I ask why you're so interested in seeing Linville's flat?' Thierry asked as the lift took them upwards.

'No real reason, I suppose,' Mac replied. 'I just think that where someone lives can tell you a lot about them. I'm interested in Linville, I'd like to know more about him, that's all.'

'Even though the case is over, even though it died with him?'

Mac shrugged.

Thierry smiled, 'Okay, now that you've mentioned it, I'm quite interested in seeing it for myself too.'

Linville's flat took up half of the top floor. The door was open and a couple of white suited forensics people were looking around it. As it wasn't a crime scene as such, they allowed them inside to have a look around so long as they wore plastic covers on their shoes and latex gloves.

Most of the flat seemed to be comprised of a huge living room. Paintings hung at regular intervals around the stark white walls. Mac couldn't help feeling that it was more like a museum than a place where someone lived. Mac stopped and looked at one of the paintings. It was an abstract and he couldn't even tell if it was the right way up.

'I take it that none of these are stolen?' Mac asked.

'No, one of Linville's hobbies was buying paintings from unknown artists. He was good at spotting up and coming talent and he often made a nice profit when he sold the paintings on,' Thierry replied.

'It makes you wonder why he had to resort to stealing then, doesn't it? I suppose he was like a lot of criminals, he just liked the excitement.'

The room was dominated by a large screen, not a TV screen, but a white screen for a projector. Mac looked up and he could see a small projector attached to the ceiling. In front of the screen there was a sofa and a low coffee table. The book lay open on the table. Apart from a cabinet against the wall this was the sum total of the furniture in the room. Thierry went over to the cabinet and turned on the DVD player. Suddenly the screen sprang to life and they saw a gigantic Professor Halvorsen introduce himself and then identify the painting, all in surround-sound. It truly was a home cinema.

The Professor disappeared. Thierry's face showed that he was impressed.

The kitchen was surprisingly small and, like the living room, everything was pristine and in its place. Mac opened the small fridge, it was empty. The bedroom had a double bed with a small cabinet beside it and a single chair. Mac opened the walk-in wardrobe. Ranks of suits were lined up ranging in colour from light grey to black. There were ties, white shirts, socks and under-wear in the drawers, all new and still in their packaging. Several shoe boxes were on the floor. Mac opened a couple of them. Each box contained a pair of black men's lace up shoes, they all looked brand new.

'You know, I can't shake off the feeling that this is more like a movie set than anything else. I don't get any sense that someone actually lived here,' Mac said with a puzzled expression.

'Yes, me too,' Kate replied. 'It's certainly nothing like my flat that's for certain. It's far too tidy.'

'Do you have any idea how long Linville spent here on average?' Mac asked turning to look at Thierry.

'We're not sure to be honest. I've often suspected that he might have led a double life of some sort and this flat just confirms that feeling. I agree with you, it just doesn't feel right.'

'What do we know about Linville's early life?'

'He was born and brought up in a small town called Langres which is around seventy kilometres from Dijon. He had no siblings and he was schooled at home. He lived quietly with his mother until she died. He was eighteen at the time and after that he became some-thing of a recluse. His mother left him quite a bit of money so he didn't need to work. He had everything delivered and saw no-one for years until suddenly at the age of twenty-four he sold up and moved to Paris. Into this very flat actually.'

'So, no-one had any photos of Sean Bernard Linville or had met him personally for years?' Mac asked.

'That's right,' Thierry said with a knowing look.

'I see what you're getting at,' Kate said. 'So, we can't even be sure that the man outside really is Sean Bernard Linville. It would be easy enough to do away with the real Linville and then take over his identity.'

'That's exactly what we were thinking. However, the only problem is that we have absolutely no proof. In fact, after all that work, we have absolutely nothing at all. Not on Linville and most definitely not on Cardini,' Thierry said in a thoroughly dejected tone of voice.

Mac couldn't help feeling a little down as well but he decided to try and be as positive as he could in the circumstances.

'Anyway, we might as well give the place a thorough going over as we're here. You never know what we might find.'

Thierry smiled and said, 'Yes you're right. We still need to do our job.'

Together with the forensics team they did as thorough a search of the flat as possible. It didn't take all that long. They found absolutely nothing. Well almost nothing.

Thierry stared hard at a small white receipt. He was staring because the print had faded and was quite hard to read. It had been found screwed up in the waste bin in the kitchen. Not the plastic bag lining the bin, which was empty, but in the bottom of the bin itself.

Mac and Dan waited patiently for Thierry to speak.

'It's for chewing gum, bought a couple of weeks ago,' Thierry said. 'What's really interesting though is where the chewing gum was bought.'

'Why is that?' Mac asked.

'Well, it's not exactly around the corner from here. It was bought in a shop on the Avenue Jean Jaures in the 19th Arrondissement, in a commune called Le Pré-Saint-Gervais which is to the north-east of Paris. It's about five miles from here, I'd guess,' Thierry replied.

'What's that part of Paris like?' Mac asked.

'Well, nothing like this that's for sure,' Thierry replied. 'From what I remember it's got lots of high-rise flats and its fair share of immigrants.'

'Is it a high crime area?' Mac asked wondering if that might be why Linville was buying gum in the area.

'No not really, it's just ordinary, an ordinary working-class part of the city,' Thierry said as he looked around the palatial space of a flat that might have easily housed at least two or three families. 'That being so, what would someone who lived in a flat like this be doing in Le Pré-Saint-Gervais?'

Thierry looked again at the receipt.

'Let's go and find out, shall we?' he said with a smile.

Chapter Nineteen

This time the police driver left the siren off and drove at a reasonable speed for which Mac was very grateful. He watched as the grand buildings of central Paris gave way to more humble houses and blocks of flats but, in truth, he found these even more interesting. This is where the majority of Parisians lived and worked and the illusion of it all being a movie set had gone. This was real and on a scale of life that Mac could relate to.

He saw a sign for the Avenue Jean Jaures and he looked out at the passing shops, work places and flats even more intently. The one thing he could honestly say about any part of Paris he'd been to was how clean it was. There were no litter or overflowing bins and he wondered how they did it.

The car pulled up outside a small grocery shop that had fruit in boxes displayed outside. Kate joined Thierry as he walked into the shop while Mac waited in the car. He knew that he'd have nothing to contribute to any conversation in French. He sighed and, not for the first time, wished that he'd taken the time to learn the language.

He looked closely at Thierry's and Kate's faces when they emerged from the shop a few minutes later. They were both smiling. They'd found something!

Thierry climbed in the front seat and turned to Mac, 'We definitely got a reaction when I showed him a picture of Linville. He said that he was sure he'd seen someone just like him in the shop quite a few times before. Unfortunately, he didn't know his name.'

'So, what do we do now?' Mac asked.

'There's a boulangerie on the corner that's also a coffee shop,' Thierry said. 'The shop owner said that he'd seen Linville in there having breakfast quite recently.'

They drove on until Thierry ordered the driver to stop outside the bakery. He and Kate then got out. They returned a few minutes later with even bigger smiles on their faces. Thierry waved at him to come out of the car.

'The baker recognised him,' Kate told Mac. 'She said that he works at a small company on the Rue Danon which is literally just around the corner. She said that it supplies all sorts of spy equipment.'

Mac followed them around the corner. They walked for about a hundred yards before Thierry stopped in front of a low pink-coloured building outside of which there was a sign that said 'Espionnage et Surveillance Internationale'. There was no door at the front of the building and no window either just a large block of glass bricks set into the front wall. To the right of the building there was a solid metal gate with spikes on the top. Mac noticed the CCTV cameras. There was one on either side of the gate and two on the roof looking down the street in opposite directions. It all looked pretty impregnable.

'I'm going to call for a team to get us in...' Thierry was saying until he was interrupted by Kate.

She had a hand against the gate and quite easily pushed the gate open.

'This is all far too easy,' Mac said sensing that something wasn't right.

'I agree,' Thierry said. 'Linville always was a tricky customer so God knows what he might have waiting for us inside. Come on, let's get back to the car. It's not worth taking any chances.'

Mac had only taken six or seven steps towards the car when he felt a twinge of pain in his back and leant against the wall of the building for a moment's respite. He then heard a sound so loud that it was noiseless. He felt a pulse of air pressure that was like someone shoving him hard in the back. Luckily, he was able to keep on his feet as he was protected from the blast by the building he was leaning against. Mac turned around fearing the worst.

177

Thierry had been behind Mac and Kate had been behind him. Mac guessed that both of them must have caught more of the blast's force. Thierry was standing about three yards away from Mac. He had his phone in his hand and a look of shock on his face. Otherwise he looked okay. Behind him the solid metal gates were now hanging off their hinges and a cloud of acrid smoke was billowing through them. He couldn't see Kate at all and he had to wait a few moments until the smoke cleared a little.

When he finally caught sight of her Mac's heart dropped into his boots. She was lying on the ground, her legs trapped underneath her body.

She wasn't moving.

Chapter Twenty

Mac tried to rush over to her but the police driver ran past him and beat him to it. He bent down and felt for a pulse. His smile told Mac that there was one. He examined her as closely as he could and then moved her gently into the recovery position and felt for a pulse again. He said something to Thierry who, like Mac, still seemed to be in shock.

'He says that her pulse is strong, Mac. I don't think she's seriously injured. She's been very lucky. I think that maybe the gate saved her from the worst of the blast.'

Mac looked around at the debris strewn across the road and knew what he meant. Any chunk of that hitting her could have been fatal. Thierry made his call. When he'd finished, he told Mac what was said.

'I've told Vincent what's happened and he's on his way. I've also told him that we'll need some medical help.'

To Mac's relief a paramedic on a motorcycle arrived a few minutes later and Thierry waved at him furiously to go over to Kate.

They could hear Vincent and his team well before they could see them. The cacophony of sirens came closer and closer until a swarm of police cars and vans arrived a few minutes later. A concerned looking Vincent climbed out of one of them. Mac could see his concern grow when he spotted Kate down on the ground. The paramedic worked on Kate while Mac, Thierry and Vincent looked on.

'Good God, I wasn't expecting this!' Vincent said as he looked around at the gates blown off their hinges and the debris strewn across the road.

Mac said nothing. The bit of him that wasn't in shock was praying furiously that Kate might be okay. The paramedic said something to Vincent.

'He says that she's unconscious but he can't find any other injuries. He thinks that she might just be concussed,' Vincent said.

Mac stopped praying. He'd gratefully settle for that.

A bright red and yellow ambulance arrived and they immediately wheeled a stretcher out. They gently lifted Kate onto it and then a doctor checked her over again. He agreed with the paramedic that there seemed to be no serious injuries but he said that she'd need to be kept in hospital for a while for observation and tests.

Kate opened her eyes as they wheeled her towards the ambulance. Mac could see confusion in her eyes.

'What happened, Mac?' she asked.

'Some sort of bomb went off and you got caught in the blast.'

She nodded wearily and then closed her eyes again.

Vincent spoke to the doctor and then turned to Mac and Thierry.

'He wants you both to go with them in the ambulance and get checked over in hospital.'

Mac nodded. There was no way he was going to leave Kate by herself. He sought out the police driver and shook his hand first. He'd now forgiven him for the fast driving and the sirens. He found that he needed some help from the paramedics to climb into the ambulance. He felt even older and more feeble than usual.

'Oh, I'm okay,' Thierry protested. 'Look, there's not a scratch.'

'You're not okay,' Vincent said pointing to Thierry's hand.

A thin stream of blood ran down the back of his hand and drops were falling from his middle finger. Thierry looked at his hand and went white. Vincent had to catch him as he fainted. He shouted for help and the paramedics wheeled out another stretcher for Thierry. They carefully loaded him up and the ambulance set off.

They hooked Kate up to a monitor and a paramedic watched her vital signs. As far as Mac could tell they looked good. On the other stretcher the doctor had cut the right-hand sleeves from Thierry's jacket and shirt just below the shoulder. Mac could see that something black was embedded in Thierry's upper arm and a stream of blood was flowing around it. The doctor looked at it carefully and then shouted something to the paramedics. A few seconds later the ambulance sped up and Mac could see the external lights flashing.

'What is it?' he asked the doctor in a worried voice.

Luckily for Mac, the doctor could speak English.

'He has something in his arm. I can't tell how big it is but it's very close to an artery. I can't touch it because he might start bleeding very badly if I do. He'll need to go into theatre as soon as we reach the hospital.'

Mac hoped that Thierry would be okay. He'd only known him for a short time but, in that time, he'd grown to like him.

It probably only took a few minutes to get to the hospital but it felt much longer. The whole scene felt so unreal that once again Mac began to wonder if he was in one of his lucid dreams. Looking at Thierry and Kate he could only hope that he was.

He began to wonder if it might have all been his fault. If he hadn't insisted on going up to Linville's flat then this might not have happened. He supposed that forensics would have found the receipt anyway but they definitely wouldn't have gone rushing over to Le Pré-Saint-Gervais just in time to get themselves blown up.

If, if, if.

He then remembered the reaction of his old boss Rob Graveley when a case had gone spectacularly wrong and Mac had started questioning himself about it. Rob always said that 'if' was the worst weasel word in the English language.

'You can worry yourself sick about 'What if I'd done this or what if I'd done that' but it won't change a thing and it helps no-one,' Rob had said to Mac. 'Bad things happen and that's it. Whatever you do don't ever let that bastard of a word 'if' enter your head. Just deal with what *is* and you'll be doing your job right.'

Mac decided to once again follow his sage advice.

When they reached the hospital, they wheeled Thierry out first and almost ran with the stretcher down the long hallway. Mac knew that it must be bad. He stayed with Kate. She was still asleep. At least he hoped it was sleep.

They wheeled Kate's stretcher in another direction and Mac followed in a wheelchair that was pushed by a nurse. They took Kate into a room where they carefully moved her from the stretcher into a hospital bed. A rack of various monitors was positioned on one side of the bed. The nurses busied themselves hooking Kate up to the monitors. One started going 'bleep' at regular intervals, a heart monitor Mac guessed. A doctor came into the room and said something to Mac. He didn't understand a word she said.

'Are you English?' the doctor asked.

'Yes, I'm sorry but I don't speak much French,' Mac said feeling both helpless and embarrassed by his lack of language skills.

'That's okay,' the doctor said. 'We'll need to carefully examine your friend to ensure that there aren't any hidden injuries. Once we've done that then we'll carefully monitor her just in case she exhibits any signs of brain damage.'

'Brain damage?' Mac said feeling sick at the thought. 'Is that likely?'

'Don't be too worried, it's just a precaution. We'll know more once we've monitored her for a while. We'll need to examine you as well. There's a room next door, if you go in and get undressed then I'll be with you once I've finished in here.'

'I'm okay really...' Mac was about to say more but he was stopped dead by the look on the doctor's face. 'Okay, I'll just go next door then.'

Mac sat on the bed and rubbed his face with his hands. He said a few more prayers before starting to undress himself. He found it quite difficult as his back appeared to have stiffened up and it was now quite painful. Mac knew there was a very good chance that it would get worse over the next day or so but for once this didn't worry him. He could only think of Kate lying unconscious next door and Thierry who, by now, would be in the operating theatre. He felt stunned. He didn't know how long he sat there before the doctor reappeared.

'How is she?' Mac asked with urgency.

'As far as we can tell your friend doesn't look too bad. Can you tell me exactly what happened?'

Mac told her about the blast while she examined him.

'You were very lucky,' she said.

'I wouldn't say that, one of us is in the theatre and another is unconscious,' Mac replied.

'No, I meant that *you* were very lucky,' she said holding up his jacket.

He could see light coming through a long diagonal slash in the fabric just below the shoulder area.

'A little closer and you might have been killed,' the doctor said.

Suddenly the room seemed to whirl about him and he felt nauseous. He threw up into a cardboard bowl that the doctor had quickly put in front of him. Once he'd finished retching the doctor gave him a glass of water. He swilled his mouth out and spat it into the bowl. He lay back on the bed feeling exhausted.

'I'm sorry,' he said. 'I didn't see that coming.'

'It's probably just the shock but there's a chance that you might be slightly concussed too,' the doctor said. 'Get yourself into bed and I'll get a nurse to hook you up to the monitors.'

Mac surprised himself by falling deeply asleep while they were still attaching the wires to him.

Chapter Twenty One

He awoke slowly and for a while he couldn't figure out where he was or what day it was. The sound of beeping made him look to his left and he could see a rack of monitors all creating glowing electronic trails as they tracked his heart rate, respiration and blood pressure. The window to his right had the blinds shut but he could make out a faint light around the edges. He guessed that it was early morning.

Then it all came back. He began looking for a call button but he couldn't see one. Luckily, a nurse came in and saw that he was awake. She came back a short time later with a doctor. It was a different doctor to the one who had seen him before.

'Ah Mister Maguire, you're awake,' he said with a professional smile.

He took some time to look at the machines. He then said something to the nurse who left.

'How are you feeling?' the doctor asked. 'Have you had any headaches, dizziness or feelings of nausea?'

'No, I don't feel too bad apart from my back,' Mac replied.

'You have a problem with your back?'

'Yes, but unfortunately it's one that I've had for some time. Before we go on can I ask you how my colleagues are doing?'

'That is Kathleen Grimsson and Thierry Rodrigues?' the doctor asked.

'Yes, that's right,' Mac said.

He held his breath while he waited for the doctor's reply.

'Well, Kathleen Grimmson seems to be fine. I checked her out an hour or so ago and, apart from a headache, she seems to be no worse for the experience. As for M. Rodrigues he's still under sedation. He had an operation last night and I must admit that he's a very lucky man. If the object that had embedded itself in his arm had come out then he could very well have bled to death.'

Mac started breathing again.

'Can I go and see her, Kate Grimsson I mean?' Mac said.

'Sure, but I need you both to stay another night just to be on the safe side,' the doctor said. 'Now tell me about your back.'

Mac told him all the details. He knew that he was being silly but in some remote part of his brain he started hoping that the doctor might jump up and tell him that, here in France, they had a magic cure for his pain. He didn't but he did book Mac in for an MRI scan just in case. He'd had three MRI scans before and he wasn't looking forward to his fourth.

Even though he was only going next door the nurse insisted that he get into a wheelchair. Kate turned her head and smiled when he was wheeled into the room. Mac thought she looked a little pale but with Kate it was hard to tell. He took her hand in his.

'How are you feeling?' he asked.

'Oh, I'm okay. I feel a little fuzzy and I've got a headache but I've had worse hangovers to be honest. How are you?'

'Oh, I'm fine, no problem at all, well apart from the fact I have to have another MRI scan.'

'Why is that?' Kate asked looking concerned.

'Oh, it's just my back,' Mac replied. 'They just want to make sure that the blast didn't make it any worse. What do you remember about yesterday?'

She looked up at the ceiling as she spoke.

'Well, I remember pretty much everything up until the blast, I think. I remember pushing open the gate at the spy shop but everything after that is a haze.'

'We were both very lucky indeed, luckier than Thierry anyway.'

'Thierry? What's happened to him?' she asked with some concern.

Mac told her what the doctor in the ambulance had said and that he'd now had an operation and was under sedation.

'Poor Thierry, I hope that he'll be okay. He literally dodged a bullet earlier on but I suppose you don't always get lucky twice. Have they any idea what caused the blast?' Kate asked.

'No, I've not spoken to anyone yet, I wanted to make sure that you were okay first. My guess is that someone got into Linville's premises just before we arrived and that's why the gate was open. I'd also guess that Linville had somehow booby-trapped the premises and whoever had gotten in had set the bomb off. We'll just have to wait until Vincent turns up to find out if I'm right.'

After half an hour Kate started to look a little sleepy so they wheeled Mac back to his room. He felt somewhat better having seen her and having spoken to her. The fact that she could remember almost everything was a good sign, he thought. He managed to drink some orange juice and some coffee a little later on but food didn't appeal to him right then.

A flustered looking Vincent arrived a little later.

'Ah Mac, they told me that you were awake. How are you and how is Kate?'

Mac assured him that they were both fine.

'How's Thierry? Have you seen him? Is he okay?'

'Yes, I've just come from him,' Vincent replied. 'He's still under sedation and his wife is with him but they say that he'll be fine. They managed to get the piece of metal out without damaging the artery too much. All in all, it could have been much worse.'

Mac could only agree.

'So, what happened?' he asked. 'I'm assuming that Linville had booby-trapped the place?'

'You assume right,' Vincent replied, 'It turns out that Linville had a second life as an importer and exporter of spy gadgets. He was obviously pretty good at bomb making too as the blast demolished most of the building. It also turned out that you weren't the only casualties of the blast. We sent in a robot to have a look around the site, just in case Linville had any more surprises for us, and it took some photos. Here look at this.'

Vincent handed over a tablet. It showed a tangle of twisted wreckage on top of which a leg without an owner could be clearly seen. It had been severed just above the knee and, while the leg was naked, the foot still had a black motorcycle boot on it. Another photo showed a human head that had been severed just under the chin. It had a large glass shard sticking out of the right temple.

'Do the leg and the head go together?' Mac asked.

'No, they belong to two different people. We don't have any ID on them as yet but we're fairly certain that one is Linville's assassin and the other is the driver of the motorcycle. We found the motorcycle parked just down the road and we're fairly certain that it's the same one that was used as the getaway vehicle after the shooting yesterday. Luckily, we managed to get a glimpse of the assassin on video just seconds before he shot the camera out. They've done some measurements on the face and they're as certain as they can be that it's the same man.'

Mac shook his head in wonder.

'So, it looks like Linville got his revenge from the grave after all. What do you think they were doing there?'

'Well, my guess is that Cardini found out somehow that he had a fake. He's got a reputation to uphold so he made sure that Linville was killed in a very public way. I'd guess that he also wanted his money back and that's what the two men were trying to find when they visited Linville's spy shop.'

'There's a sort of rough justice there, I suppose,' Mac said. 'So, Cardini may have lost two men but otherwise it looks like he'll get away with it.'

'Yes, you're unfortunately right there,' Vincent said with a resigned shrug of the shoulders. 'Anyway, I need to get back and see where the team are up to. I'll let you know if anything happens but don't hold your breath.'

They wheeled him out for his MRI scan later that afternoon. It only lasted about twenty minutes but it felt a lot longer than that to Mac. They fed him into a cramped tube which gave him a mild case of claustrophobia and then the noises started. Even with ear plugs in the electronic pulses sounded very loud and it just got worse. Towards the end it sounded as if several very strong men were pounding the outside of the metal tube with sledgehammers. He was relieved when the noise stopped and he once again slid out towards the light.

The doctor visited him later and told him what they'd found. Mac was certain that he'd only hear what he been told every time before but he mentally kept his fingers crossed just in case.

'Well, it would appear that your condition hasn't gotten too much worse because of the blast so you've been very lucky there. Of course, your pain levels will probably rise for a while but that's only to be expected,' the doctor said.

Mac then asked the sixty four million dollar question.

'Is there anything you can do about it?'

The doctor shrugged and, almost word for word, repeated what his own neurologist had said.

'I'm sorry but there's a lot of damage down there and we can't rebuild spines just yet.'

Mac's face must have shown his disappointment.

'But don't give up, we're developing some very good pain therapies now and I'm sure that one of those will be of help before long.'

Mac thanked the doctor. At least he'd left him with a crumb of comfort. He couldn't help feeling more than a little depressed though. He started alternating between staring at the ceiling and falling into a series of light sleeps. When he finally came to it was evening and Kate was sitting beside his bed.

'How are you feeling?' Mac asked.

'I'm not too bad,' she replied. 'It really knocks you about though something like this, doesn't it?'

Mac could only agree. He tried to sit up and a bolt of pain made him wince. Kate had to help him.

'Oh well, the doctor said the pain would get worse. I shouldn't really moan though. I'd guess that we've both used up our allocation of luck for the next few years at least.'

Mac told her everything that Vincent had said earlier.

'It's a sort of justice I suppose,' she said. 'So, what happens tomorrow?'

Mac shrugged.

'We go home. From what Vincent said that's it, the case is over. I don't know about you but, personally, I think I've had about enough of this case anyway.'

This made Kate smile.

'Yes, me too,' she said. 'I love Paris but I think that, in this particular case, I'll be glad to be going home.'

Mac knew that he had told her something of a white lie. Even after everything that had happened, he still desperately wanted to find something against Cardini.

The only problem was that Linville had probably taken that knowledge to the grave with him.

Chapter Twenty Two

Mac lay in bed most of the night wishing for the morning to come. It took its time but, after several discussions with the doctors, they eventually discharged him and Kate on the proviso that they promised to see their own doctors as soon as they got back home. They took a taxi and headed straight to the Quai. They were going to drop in on Vincent's team to say their goodbyes and to see if there had been any developments. After that they were planning to head back to the hotel to pick up their things before going to the train station later that afternoon. They were going home.

Before they left the hospital, they had managed to get a few minutes with Thierry to say their goodbyes. He was conscious but still very groggy. They were able to exchange a few words with his wife Dianne too. She was an attractive woman in her thirties who somehow reminded him a little of Nora. She smiled at them but Mac could see the worry lines that had been deeply etched in her face.

At the Quai they made their way to the team's room. The last time they'd been there it had been full of excited people but now there was just a couple of the team in evidence and they weren't exactly rushing their work. Mac could sense their despondence. Vincent got up and rushed over to meet them.

'How are you both?' he asked as he gave first Mac and then Kate a hug.

'I'm fine,' Mac replied.

'Yes, me too,' Kate said.

Vincent's eyes flicked from one to the other. It was clear from his expression that he wasn't totally convinced by their words.

'Did you see Thierry before you left the hospital?' he asked.

'Yes, we did and we managed to have a few words with him too,' Mac said. 'He said that he was okay and to send you his thanks for spotting the fact that he was bleeding. If you hadn't noticed it when you did then he might well be dead by now.'

Vincent shook his head.

'It just feels so wrong, the case ending like this with Thierry in hospital, Linville dead and Cardini getting away with it.'

Mac was in the process of sadly agreeing when Christophe ran into the room. He said something to Vincent and Kate translated for Mac.

'He's very excited and says that he wants us all to look at one of the monitors.'

Mac and Kate joined them around the big screen. Christophe tapped away at the computer keyboard and an image appeared of a man sitting down.

'He says that this is a CCTV stream from the waiting room on the ground floor,' Kate explained. 'The man came in a short while ago and asked to speak to Vincent.'

The camera zoomed in on the man. He wore glasses and had a light beard but it was Linville! Mac looked again and there could be no doubt, that profile couldn't be mistaken. He wondered for a moment if he'd suffered some sort of brain damage after all.

'Vincent's ordered them to get him up here straight away,' Kate said.

A few minutes later they gathered around the screen again. It now showed the inside of an interview room. The man sat on the far side of the table while Vincent and Christophe sat on the other. Again, Kate translated what was said.

'You said that you wanted to see someone about the Linville case?' Vincent said.

The man had a sad expression on his face as he said, 'Yes I saw it on the news yesterday. Sean Linville was my brother. We're twins, or we were twins, I suppose I should say. His real name was Francois Masson. My name is Philippe Masson.'

'Tell me about your brother,' Vincent asked.

Philippe looked up to the ceiling while he gathered his thoughts.

'We were brought up in an orphanage in a small town called Saint-Marcy not far from Dijon. I still live there.'

'Why were you both in an orphanage?' Vincent asked.

'I never did find out for sure but, when I was young, I overheard one of the nuns talking about a young girl who'd been raped. When she saw me, she stopped talking and looked at me in a peculiar way.'

Philippe shrugged before he continued.

'We looked identical, Francois and I, but, even when we were young, we were very different. I always had my nose in a book while he always wanted excitement. He'd often do something stupid that would get him a beating from the nuns and I'd ask him why. He'd always say that even a beating was better than being bored. They all said that I was the intelligent one but I always knew that Francois was smarter than me in lots of ways. He just couldn't settle down and apply himself though. He said that he found the orphanage stifling.

He ran away from there when he was thirteen and I didn't get any news about him until two or three years later. The nuns said that he'd gotten arrested for burglary. I don't know what happened to him after that although I tried to find him on several occasions over the years but he obviously didn't want to be found. I didn't hear from him again until four or five years ago.

He said that, while he had been involved in the criminal world for a short time, he'd now changed his ways. He'd also changed his name. That was because he wanted to leave his former live as a criminal behind him or so he said. He'd become something of an art expert and was now buying and selling paintings and making quite a bit of money doing it. We met a few times, always in private,

193

and then he asked if I wouldn't mind looking after his flat for him for a few days from time to time. I was happy to do it for him. It was a simple enough request and I really wanted to have a relationship with my brother. After all, he was the only relative I had. He always left me his credit card and, if I'm honest, a few days eating out in some the best restaurants in Paris was no hardship either. On my salary it's something I don't get to do that often. However, I was forgetting just how manipulative Francois could be and when he said that I should wear my contact lenses while I was there, I figured that something else might be going on.'

Philippe stopped for a moment to gather his thoughts.

'In my wildest dreams I never thought that he could have been a murderer though, you have to believe that. Remembering what Francois was like I figured he might have been up to something illicit but not that.'

'What do you do?' Vincent asked.

'Me? I'm an Assistant Professor at the University in Dijon. I teach physics. Anyway, I'm happy to answer any questions you may have but this is the main reason that I'm here today.'

He pulled an envelope out of his inside pocket and slid it across the table to Vincent. It simply said 'Quand je suis mort' on the outside in neat handwriting.

'When I am dead. What's does that mean?' Vincent asked.

'Francois made me promise him that, if he should ever die, I would give this envelope to the police,' Philippe explained. 'I've no idea what's in it.'

'Christophe, can you finish the interview off and get M. Masson's details,' Vincent asked before he left the room.

He appeared in the room clutching the envelope in his hand.

'Paper opener someone,' he barked.

One of the team gave him a small paper knife. He carefully opened the envelope and shook the contents out onto the desk. There was a key and a slip of paper. Vincent read the slip of paper carefully before picking up the key and looking at it in wonder.

'It's the key to a safety deposit box. The address is that of a small private bank not far from here. He's written down everything we need to access the box,' Vincent said.

He only hung around long enough to bark out some orders before rushing out with a couple of his men.

'Do you want to hang around for a bit and see what happens?' Mac asked.

'You bet,' Kate replied with a smile. 'I wonder what could possibly be in the safety deposit box?'

'I'm really hoping that it might be some more revenge from the grave by Linville. He worked in a very risky business so it's possible that he kept some insurance. We can only hope.'

Christophe came into the room fifteen minutes later.

'He definitely knows his physics,' he said.

'What do you mean?' Mac asked.

'Well, it had occurred to me that, as they looked so alike, perhaps the evil twin had swapped places some-how. I'm into astronomy so I was able to ask him a few questions about physics, questions to which I knew the answer. He passed with flying colours. In fact, he almost gave me the full lecture on Feynman diagrams. We'll check him out further anyway just in case.'

Mac thought that they'd be very wise to do that. Linville, as he still thought of him, had been a very slippery character so it would be best to be on the safe side.

Vincent returned just over an hour later. He had a big smile on his face so he'd obviously found something.

'At first I thought that the safety deposit box was empty,' he said. 'Then I shook it and this tiny memory stick fell down. It's with our technical people now. They say that there's quite a lot of data on it, mostly around financial transactions, but there was also a video. It was titled 'Look at this first' and so we did. Here I'll show you.'

He spoke to one of his men and a grainy video appeared on the big screen. Kate translated for Mac.

The picture was very shaky to start with as the camera was obviously on someone who was walking towards a table around which three men sat. The table was set in the middle of a grassy field. When the camera got closer, they could easily identify one of the men as Cardini. At this point the sound kicked in.

'There's the small matter of the down payment first,' a voice said.

'That's Linville speaking,' Vincent explained.

A man laid an attaché case on the table and opened it up. It was full of money. A hand shut the case and it disappeared out of view.

'One million euros,' Cardini said, *'with another three million on delivery as agreed.'*

'Everything has been prepared and you can expect delivery within the next two weeks.'

'There'll be no loose ends I hope?' Cardini asked.

'I never leave any loose ends. It will be an absolutely clean job.'

Cardini and the other two men stood up and walked off. The video ended.

'By itself it might not be enough to nail Cardini but, if we can link him to the robbery and murder of Ben Meeks, then it will certainly help,' Vincent said. 'Linville was always very thorough and I've got a feeling that he'll make sure that we have more than enough to nail Cardini.'

'I take it that he used some of his spy equipment to film the meeting?' Mac asked.

'It looks like it. I know that Cardini's usually very careful so it must have been something special to get past a search. So perhaps we'll have our 'happy ever after' ending after all,' Vincent said with a smile.

'But hopefully it won't be happy ever after for Cardini though. I'm so glad we stopped by. I'll be leaving Paris with a much lighter heart,' Mac said.

'And how about you Kate?' Vincent asked. 'I hope this hasn't put you off our city?'

'No, nothing could ever do that,' Kate said giving Vincent a big smile.

'Good, so if either of you come here again please be sure to look me up. Oh, Mac I'm sorry, I was hoping to have some time free before you left but with this new evidence...'

'Don't worry about that. I'll be back before long, I promise,' Mac said. 'Please give Sylvie my best too.'

'Good, I'll hold you to your promise,' Vincent said before he hugged Mac again and kissed him on both cheeks. He then did the same to Kate.

The trip home would have been something akin to torture for Mac if he'd have been alone. Luckily, he wasn't and he and Kate talked for most of the trip back which helped to take his mind off the pain.

'Do you know what I find so interesting?' Kate said. 'Here we have two identical twins, brought up in exactly the same environment, yet they turn out so completely different. Why is that do you think?'

Mac gave it some thought.

'Yes, why did one twin become an academic while the other turned into a thief and a murderer? Even Philippe Masson himself didn't seem to understand how that had happened. I don't know, perhaps it just takes something really small to happen to start sending one person down a different road to another. Once you've started down that road, for some people at least, it seems like there's no turning back.'

'Yes, I suppose we take decisions all the time that send us down one road or another,' Kate said.

'Tell me about your road,' Mac asked.

Kate sighed and closed her eyes for a moment before replying.

'I've often heard people talk about a sense of belonging. I've never experienced that. In school I didn't have many friends because some of the children said that I must be a witch because I looked so odd. I almost began to believe it myself at one time. When I was in England, I was told that I was Irish because I had a slight accent from my mother, while in Ireland they said that I was English and in Iceland I don't think they knew what I was, apart from not being Icelandic of course. I was always something else, something different to everyone else.'

Mac was beginning to understand her. He could understand her loneliness too.

She then told him about her father who was a banker and someone who had just about ruined the Icelandic economy when his bank failed. About how he'd actually made money on the failure by betting against the bank and how he still felt no remorse for what he'd done. She told him about her mother who had died ashamed of the man she'd married and about her brother who had fled to the other end of the earth to get away from his father. She told him about being a barrister in training before packing it all up to join the police when her mother died, a move that she knew would annoy the hell out of her father.

'And you've not spoken to him since, your father?' Mac asked.

Kate shook her head.

'I don't want to, ever,' she said with absolute certainty.

'Have you had any second thoughts since joining the force? After all you could be earning a lot more as a barrister.'

198

She looked out of the window as she gave this question some thought.

'If I'm being honest, I liked the law but I'd guess that it wouldn't have taken long before I'd have gotten bored with it. The one thing that you can say about being in the police is that it's definitely not boring and, after all, I'm kind of working in the same area anyway, aren't I?'

She looked out of the window again but all that was beyond it was the blackness of the tunnel and her reflection in the glass. It seemed appropriate somehow.

'I'm sorry Mac,' she said.

'Sorry? What for?'

'For burdening you with all my sorrows. I've realised that the only thing in life that that I've excelled at lately is being miserable.'

'Isn't there someone in your life?' Mac asked. 'Someone you can talk to?'

'No, not since I got divorced and God knows we didn't talk all that much when we were married anyway. So, there's only my brother and he's living in South Africa which is not exactly around the corner. No, I might just as well get used to being alone I suppose.'

He wished that he could do something to help her but all he could do is offer her some words.

'Something will happen Kate, something good, just wait and see. Life can be a bloody nightmare sometimes but now and again it produces something wonderful and unexpected. It did for me when I met my Nora. I hope it does for you too one day.'

For the first time since they left Paris Kate smiled. She reached over and gave his hand a squeeze.

It was just a short walk to Kings Cross from St. Pancras but it still proved very painful for Mac although he was careful not to let Kate see it. Luckily, she was still wrapped up in her own thoughts. As the train made its way back to Letchworth, he felt every bump and curve on the track. He did his best to disguise his discomfort and he could relax a little when Kate got off the train at Hatfield.

He caught a taxi back home. Although it was still early evening, he left his bag in the hallway, undressed and went straight to bed. He knew that he was going to be in for a bad night so he took the 'nuclear option' as he'd nicknamed it. This consisted of two small blue tablets that, when taken, would guarantee unconsciousness for at least twelve hours.

In this case they worked for a little less than that as he woke at five o'clock the next morning. He'd been having a lucid dream but when he awoke the dream drained out of his mind like water through his hands. All he could remember was that he was being chased by a dog or he was chasing a dog, he wasn't sure which, but a dog was definitely involved. He knew that he wouldn't be able to get back to sleep anytime soon so he decided to get up and make some coffee.

He gingerly stood up and decided that the pain, while still having an edge to it, was just about bearable. He filled the bird feeders and then looked out of the window as he sipped his coffee. He thought while he did this.

The Meeks case was closed. They now knew who had killed him and who had paid for it to happen. He'd follow the rest of the Cardini case as best he could from this side of the channel but it was all up to Vincent and his team now. He had every hope that the evidence Linville had supplied them with from his grave would be more than enough to put Cardini behind bars.

On remembering that he'd totally missed yesterday evening, Mac checked his phone. He had one message, time stamped at seven in the evening, and it was from Johnny Kinsella.

'Hi Mac, the wife's going filming in a couple of days so I was wondering if you and your friend would like to come over and have a few beers.' There was a slight pause.

'It would be really nice to catch up on the old days. I'm already looking forward to it. Give me a ring.'

And he sounded like he was too. When Mac had first met Johnny there was a definite note of sadness in his voice. He'd thought that maybe it was just how he spoke but, listening to him on the phone, he now realised that he'd been wrong. He texted Johnny back and confirmed that he and Tim would definitely be there. He didn't need to ask Tim if he was free, he knew he'd drop everything for the chance of an evening with Johnny Kinsella. He texted Tim and gave him the good news.

What a nice way to start a day, Mac thought.

He glanced out of the kitchen window. In the half morning light, he could see a little flock of Coal Tits taking turns at the bird feeders and on the ground a solitary Robin Redbreast was pecking away at the seeds he'd scattered there. He saw a movement behind the Robin. It was next door's cat creeping upon the bird and it had its cruel hunter's face on. Mac rattled the door knob as hard as he could and the birds went flying in all directions while the cat slunk back into its own garden. He knew that it was just the cat's nature but that didn't make him like the cat any more. Once again, the idea of having a dog popped into his head.

He refilled his cup with coffee and then pondered the idea of getting a dog quite seriously. He looked out at his garden. It had hedges around most of it and a secure high fence at the back, there might just be one bit where he might need to put some extra wire fencing up. He stopped still as a sudden thought hit him.

He needed to speak to Adil Thakkar urgently but it was still only five twenty in the morning. The thought went scurrying around in his head and he knew that he'd have no peace until he settled the matter. He finished his coffee and got dressed, remembering to put his set of lock picks in his jacket pocket.

By six o'clock he was standing outside Albert Ginn's front door doing a spot of breaking and entering. It was something that he would never have considered doing when he was in the force and he supposed that this was one of the few benefits of his now being a civilian. It wasn't the house he was interested in but the garden. He made his way out of the garden door onto the lawn and started to carefully examine the fence panels separating Albert Ginn's garden from Mrs. Dellow's next door.

The fence was very sturdy and, although he examined each panel carefully, he didn't find what he'd been looking for. He took a step back and looked down the length of the fence and noticed that the panel roughly in the middle of the garden wasn't quite as long as the others. Of course, this could be easily explained. If you started the fence from either end of the garden with full sized panels then the middle one was very unlikely to be the same size as the other panels but he still wondered.

He went back and examined this panel once again but he found nothing different except that this one had a large, round knot near one side. He looked at it more closely but it still seemed entirely natural. So, he was surprised when he touched it to hear a soft click. The panel moved away from him at one end by about a quarter of an inch. He put his hand to the panel and it swung smoothly open like a door. He walked into next door's garden and, through the kitchen window, he could see Mrs. Dellow at her sink. She was filling a kettle. She glanced out of the window and, when she saw him, she froze for a second before waving at him to come in.

'Cup of tea, dear?' she asked with a bright smile as Mac closed the kitchen door behind him.

'Yes, why not?' he replied feeling how surreal the situation was.

'I knew that someone would find it eventually. I was just hoping that I would have a few hours more. Oh well,' she said with a resigned smile.

'Why do you need a few hours more?' Mac asked.

'I'm signing the documents for the house sale at two o'clock this afternoon and, once I've done that, then I won't mind very much what happens to me.'

'Why is selling the house so important to you?'

'It's not for me, it's for my sister, my little sister. Of course, she's nearly sixty now but she's still my little sister to me and she's not had a good life. Like me she's been saddled with an unnatural husband, mine was a cruel trickster, hers was a violent drunk. It was the best day of her life when he was struck down by a heart attack and died. She's always had this dream of us both selling our houses and opening a little tea shop in Devon, just the two of us. I'm afraid that it will just be her now but I want her to have her dream.'

At that point the dog came in and, spotting Mac, he started growling again.

'Terry, get back in your box,' Mrs. Dellow said with authority. The dog scampered off. 'It was him that gave me away, wasn't it?'

'Yes. I never thought to ask my police colleague if he'd given you the dog to look after but, when I finally thought about it, I considered it unlikely. If a dog is found without its owner it's normal practice to take it to the pound first. So, I wondered if there was another way the dog could have gotten into your garden. Was it your husband that built the secret door?'

'Yes, he was good with his hands I'll give him that. He used it whenever someone he didn't like turned up, usually a friend of mine or the vicar. He'd just say he was going into the garden and then he'd disappear next door and drink whisky with that hateful cousin of his and chortle about the great joke.'

'Tell me what happened,' Mac asked gently.

'I was out in the garden as I said when I heard the argument start. I opened the secret door and crept up to Albert's house so I could hear what was being said a little better. I thought that Father Curran was absolutely excellent. He said exactly what I've wanted to say to that horrid man for so many years. Then there was a struggle for the gun which thankfully Father Curran won. He placed it in the corner just by the door, no more than a few feet away from where I was hiding. I found that I couldn't take my eyes of it. All of the little cruelties that hideous man had perpetrated during his lifetime ran through my head like some mad sort of film. All I can remember is Father Curran leaving the room, then there was a loud bang and there I was standing over Albert's dead body. I threw the gun down and ran out into the garden. I didn't have time to make it back into my garden as Father Curran came back into the room so I hid out of sight around the corner.

When he'd gone, I went back into my own garden closing the secret door behind me and then I tried to think. It was wrong of me but I could only think of my sister and how, with that man dead, I could finally sell the house. I honestly didn't believe that they would charge Father Curran. I convinced myself that they would call it suicide and so I dialled 999. It was only after I'd finished the call that I noticed that Terry was in my garden. He must have run through the secret door when he heard the noise of the gun going off. The poor thing was quite frightened. I couldn't chance opening the door again as the police might turn up and so I kept him. Even though Albert was trying to teach him to be nasty he really is a sweet little dog so it was no hardship. The rest you know.'

'I take it that you still had your gardening gloves on when you shot Albert Ginn? There were no fingerprints on the gun other than Father Curran's and Albert's.'

She nodded.

204

'I didn't think about it at the time though. I wasn't thinking logically or at all if I'm honest. I'd fantasised so many times about doing something just like that to both Albert and my husband, sometimes a knife, sometimes poison, whatever took my fancy really, but mostly it was with a gun. My father taught me to shoot so I knew what to do. It was just a little game I used to play with myself to help keep me sane. I thought I was fantasising again until I heard the bang. I was quite shocked at what I'd done if I'm honest.'

'You know that you've allowed an innocent man to go through hell these past few days?' Mac said.

'I know that all too well, Mr. Maguire, and it was very bad of me but what else could I do? Here was my one chance to sell my house and give my poor sister the life she'd always dreamt of. She's an innocent person too, a person who's been tortured for years and she deserves a little happiness before she goes. Father Curran is a true Christian, I know that he'll forgive me,' she said as she stood up. 'I'd better get dressed, I suppose, if we're going to the police station.'

Mac thought for a while and then shook his head.

'I'm not in the police force anymore, Mrs. Dellow. Look, I'll forget that I ever found that door if you go to the police and hand yourself in as soon as you've signed the papers to sell your house.'

'Thank you, thank you so much Mr. Maguire, you're a true Christian too. I'll go straight to the station as soon as the papers are signed, I promise.' She looked around the kitchen. 'It looks nice here, doesn't it? It isn't though. What was it they used to say on that soap? Yes, that's it, kippers and curtains. It's been kippers and curtains for me ever since my husband died. Unfortunately, he didn't invest wisely and I was left with very little money. Last winter I could either eat or keep the house heated but not both and, on some days, I couldn't afford either. I've had a miserable existence these last few years but one

205

must keep up appearances, mustn't one? Can I ask you a question?'

'Of course,' Mac replied.

'What's jail like? Is it kept heated, do they feed you?' she asked.

'Oh yes. It's heated and they give you three meals a day.'

'Three meals every day? Now there's a wonder. I'd guess you'd always have some company too, someone to talk to?'

'Yes, I think you could guarantee that.'

'They don't make you work, do they? You know breaking rocks, sewing mailbags and the like?' she asked with a frown.

'No, they haven't done that for years.'

She gave Mac a beatific smile, 'Well, that doesn't sound too bad then, does it? I think me and jail might get on very well. There's just one problem, the dog. He's really very nice.'

'I'm sorry Mrs. Dellow but that's one thing I definitely can't help you with.'

Mac felt that he shouldn't keep his client in suspense for a minute longer. He knocked next door and luckily Father Pat was up and just about to have breakfast. He invited Mac to eat with him and, as he was having bacon and eggs, Mac felt that he could find it in him to keep the priest company. While he was cooking Mac told the priest about his conversation with Mrs. Dellow. As always, the priest's first thoughts were always for others.

'That poor, poor woman. If I'd only known about the privations she'd been suffering. If only I hadn't argued so and then placed the gun within such easy reach...'

'Don't blame yourself Father,' Mac said. 'She was very good at keeping up appearances and you weren't to know she was even there, let alone what she'd do. I think it was just the last straw for her.'

'What do you think will happen to her?'

Mac thought for a moment.

'She'll get jail but there may be some extenuating circumstances and, as she looks like everyone's favourite granny, they might go easy on her.'

'I just wish that there was something I could do for her,' the priest said.

'There is Father.'

'What's that, Mac?'

'Forgive her.'

'That I will, the poor woman. I'll go around straight after we've eaten and speak to her.'

'Thanks Father, and if you want to do me a big favour, act surprised when the police tell you.'

'I'll do my best Mac, I promise.'

As he walked back towards the car Mac found that he was moved by Father Pat's words and thought that the world could do with a few more like him. He opened his car door and glanced sideways at his passenger as he sat down.

'Don't start getting too comfortable,' he warned. 'This is only a temporary arrangement.'

Mac stopped along the way to get a few necessities. He was planning a little party for himself and Tim that evening.

Chapter Twenty Three

Kate hadn't slept well. She'd dreamt a lot during the night and the dreams were all dark and foreboding. She was up early and she decided to go into the station to see what was going on. Everyone had questions for her so she sat down and brought Dan and the whole team up to speed with everything that had happened in Paris, well almost everything. Dan was happy as the case was now closed out. Yet another win for the team.

'And how's Mac?' Dan asked. 'I was expecting him to call in today too.'

'And here I am,' a voice said from the doorway.

'Mac!' Dan said. 'It sounds like you had an exciting time in Paris.'

'A bit too exciting for me, if I'm honest. It was a close call, too bloody close,' Mac said as he turned to Kate. 'Are you okay?'

'I'm fine. I'm still a bit tired that's all,' she replied.

'I'll bet that she didn't tell you that she was knocked unconscious by the bomb, did she?' Mac asked.

From the look on the team's faces he could tell that she hadn't.

'Kate, you really should take a few days off,' Dan said.

'I'd sooner be here if that's okay. I've got no-one at home.'

'Okay, I suppose it's better that you're with someone just in case you have some sort of reaction but look after yourself and don't take on too much,' Dan ordered.

Kate nodded.

'So, what are you going to do now then, Mac?' Dan asked.

'Well, it's back to the office for me.' He thought back to the beginning of the case and when he'd met Ben Meeks outside his office door. 'You never know, I might have a client waiting for me. Anyway, whatever happens I'll be nicely tucked up in the Magnets with my friend Tim in a couple of hours. I've got quite a story to tell him too. You can join us if you want Kate. I'm doing dinner around eight as well, it's steak and potatoes if you're interested.'

'Thanks Mac. I'm really tempted but I think that I'll go straight home tonight if you don't mind,' Kate replied. 'I'm still feeling a little tired.'

Kate tried to concentrate on completing some paper work but she couldn't keep her mind on the job. The day dragged by alleviated only by Adil's news that Mrs. Dellow had come into the station and confessed to being Albert Ginn's murderer. That was a real surprise to everyone. Adil said that he'd rang Mac with the news but, for some reason, he got the feeling it wasn't that much of a surprise to him.

Dan was beaming as yet another case was more or less closed.

Kate watched the hands of the clock go slowly around. She found that she couldn't concentrate at anything. She was just about to give up and go home when Jo breezed in.

She looked both happy and excited and Kate felt a mild tinge of jealousy. Jo made her way around the team, chatting to each of them in turn. It was all about the wedding of course. Around the station they'd dubbed it 'The Wedding of the Century'. Calling it that had, at first, been a bit of a joke but, as the date grew nearer, they'd all gotten caught up in the preparations. As everyone in the station who could make it was going to be there, it was becoming quite a big deal.

'Ah, Kate,' Jo said when it was her turn. 'I hope that you'll be there at the weekend?'

'Well, I was hoping to be there but I wasn't sure. I haven't had an invitation as yet.'

'Yes, I'm sorry that was my fault,' Jo said. 'I forgot with everything that was going on and then I ran out of invitations. I was going to write a note but then I thought that I'd pop into the station and invite you personally. I should think that you could do with some light relief after all the excitement you've been having.'

'Thanks Jo, I'm looking forward to it already,' Kate said with a smile.

'Well, make sure that you get to the front of the crowd when I throw the bouquet. You never know but it might be your turn next,' Jo said with a wink.

Kate appreciated the sentiment but she doubted that such a day would ever come again. She'd tried it once before and it had been a disaster.

'Is everyone from the station coming?' Kate asked without meaning to or really understanding why. 'I mean the local detective team, are they all invited too?'

'Oh yes and they've all said that they're coming as well. Why are you interested in one of them?'

Kate didn't reply but her face said enough.

'Well, I won't pry but I have to admit that, even though I'm deeply in love with the finest man in the world, I couldn't help noticing that a couple of them are quite fit, if you know what I mean,' Jo said with a glint in her eye. 'So, just keep your fingers crossed that they don't get a spate of robberies or something in the meantime.'

'Thanks Jo, you've really cheered me up.'

And she had. Kate stood up and gave Jo a hug and wished her all the best for the wedding.

She went home a little earlier than usual. She thought about what Jo had said as she looked out of the train window. She didn't know what was happening to her. Her whole life was a total mess and it was only work that kept her sane these days. She felt as if she was empty inside. She looked around the carriage. There were several couples travelling together, some chatting, some holding hands and some just sitting together. She envied them all.

She felt lonely all the time and she was getting tired of that too. Perhaps she might have a go at catching Jo's bouquet after all.

Chapter Twenty Four

Mac smiled as he dished their dinner up. He'd cooked one of his favourite meals, steak in onion gravy, and luckily it was also one of Tim's favourites too. It wasn't often that he found the energy to cook a meal from scratch but he felt the successful outcome of Father Pat's case deserved a little celebration. He'd cooked more steak than he needed just in case Kate turned up. This meant that his other guest also got a good portion. He wolfed down in a few seconds even though he'd not long eaten.

Over dinner he continued telling Tim all about his adventures in Paris and about Kate too. Even he had to admit that it was quite a story. After that they started discussing their upcoming 'boy's night in' with Johnny Kinsella. Tim was so excited at the prospect of meeting one of his musical heroes. Mac had the feeling that it was truly going to be a night to remember.

After dinner Mac got out the Howling Wolf album and placed it reverentially on the turntable. He knew that he'd have to return it to Johnny soon so a final listen to the album was a must. He turned the lights down low and got a cold can of beer for each of them and started the record off. He had a CD of the album and he knew every word of each song by heart. This was different though. This was vinyl and something that had once belonged to the Wolf himself. It sounded as though Wolf and his band were playing right there in his living room. When it came to the third track and the familiar riff the hairs on Mac's neck stood up and he felt some of the excitement he'd felt when he'd first heard it in Charlie's Blues House. Then the Wolf started howling.

'Oh, Smokestack lightning, shining just like gold,

Why don't you hear me crying, whoo hoo, whoo hoo hoo, whoo hoo.'

Mac sang along and howled with the Wolf. Terry sat up in his basket and started howling too.

'What do you know?' Tim said looking at Terry in some surprise. 'A dog that likes the blues. Perhaps you two might get on after all.'

Eight months later

BBC News website –
'The trial of Matthieu Cardini, who has been dubbed a European 'super-criminal', has just ended in Paris. He has been found guilty of murder, theft and money laundering. He showed no reaction at the verdict. He will be sentenced later but the judge intimated that he would be likely to receive the highest penalty possible, in this case life imprisonment. M. Cardini's role in the theft of actress Cathy Conyers' painting came to light after the death of the art thief Francois Masson, who was known as Sean Linville at the time. Masson left behind a mass of evidence that would not only help to incriminate Cardini but many of his associates as well.

By coincidence Miss Conyers was also in the news again as she was pictured yesterday handing over her painting by Edvard Munch to the National Gallery. She said that she'd decided that something so beautiful deserved to be seen by everyone. The ceremony was a family affair as it was also attended by her rock star husband Johnny Kinsella and his daughter and son-in-law Roisin and Daniel Kavanagh who are expecting their first child next month.

The End

I hope that you enjoyed this story. If you have then please leave a review and let me know what you think.
PCW

Also in the Mac Maguire series

The Body in the Boot

The Dead Squirrel

The Weeping Women

The Blackness

23 Cold Cases

The Match of the Day Murders

The Chancer

The Tiger's Back

The Eight Bench Walk

https://patrickcwalshauthor.wordpress.com/

Made in the USA
Las Vegas, NV
20 May 2022

49146111R00132